KING PIANKHI

The First Black Pharaoh of Egypt

Written and Edited

by

Michael K. Jones

Cover picture is the Meroe Pyramids in Sudan.

Revised in 2019. (Michael's Awakening 2017)

This is a work of fiction. All events and characters in this story are solely the product of the author's imagination. Any similarities between any characters and situations presented in this book to any individuals, living or dead, or actual places and situations are purely coincidental.

ISBN-13: 978-1979012041
ISBN-10: 1979012040

www.excursionthemovie.com

CHAPTERS

PROLOGUE

Many centuries ago, the first descendants of African people willingly migrated to countries all around the world. As we all know much later in time, many who were black Hebrews, were forced to relocate not of their own free will. Those scattered Israelites that were enslaved learned to adapt and blend into their newly adopted societies in order to survive. And even though they contributed significantly in the development of their new nations; whether politically, socially, or scientifically, they are not recognized in the history teachings of their adopted countries.

The Kushite Kingdom of Nubia which is now Sudan invaded and ruled over Egypt from 730 BC to 656 BC. The thought of Egyptians being conquered by black Africans for almost 75 years is an embarrassment to them. They perceive the Nubians as subservient (less important) and inferior. To this day they will not acknowledge their own history during the 25th dynasty.

When Egypt ruled Nubia early on in time and discovered they had gold, they forcefully took control of their lucrative mines. Precious metals were not prominent in North Africa, and ambassadors of other conquered countries were persuaded to bring the ruling pharaohs gifts of their gold to prove their loyalty.

The Kushites also presented the pharaohs with ivory, ostrich feathers, fruits, exotic products and a variety of wild animals including giraffes.

During the reign of Pharaoh Amenhotep III (18th dynasty) he married a local woman in Nubia named Tiy to strengthen his rule over the two countries.

The Egyptians of today will not acknowledge this and even deny that Queen Tiy was black. She was the mother of Akhenaten who later married several wives including Nefertiti, whom some believe was his sister because of their famous club foot child Tutankhamen. (Sept. 2010 National Geographic Issue)

Another part of Egyptian history later deleted was the Second Turko-Egyptian War. In 1841, Egypt was defeated by the Ottoman Empire in Syria and Crete. They were later forced to release their control of the two countries. (Ottoman Wars 1700 to 1870)

In 1948, the United Nations, under the orders from the richest (Jewish) men in the world, recognized Israel as a sovereign country. In retaliation for the decision, a number of Arab nations decided to attack beginning the Arab-Israeli War of 1948. Almost a year later, Egypt in 1949 was the first Arab country to embarrassingly sign an armistice with Israel.

The Arab-Israeli War of 1967 is one of the most humiliating conflicts in Egyptian history. Syria, Jordan, and Egyptian forces surrounded the nation of Israel. Knowing an attack was eminent, Israel striked first defeating the military of all three Arab countries in only six days, taking and keeping the city of Jerusalem.

Again in 1973, Syrian and Egyptian forces unsuccessfully attacked Israel knowing they would be vulnerable during their most religious day, Yom Kippur. The war only lasted nine days in which Israel's Navy distinguished itself by sinking 34 enemy vessels; included were Egyptian missile and torpedo boats.

Chapter One

2010

Driving all night, two Range Rovers and a van full of hired local help sped southbound down a long endless paved road as the red hot sun continued to rise. They suddenly turned left and veered onto the desert sand as fear fell upon the face of the lead driver. He knew time was running out and the base camp had to be set up before the desert temperatures rose to unbearable levels.

Anand rode in the second vehicle and was excited to be on the archeological expedition to the Meroe Pyramids in Sudan. He was the only black on the team as an Arabic translator and hieroglyphics interpreter. The lead archaeologist Dr. Joe Ember personally picked Anand a month ago in the capital city of Khartoum Sudan. What the doctor didn't know was…he chose him.

Anand was twenty five years old and born in Khartoum Sudan. The only way to get permission from the Sudanese government to excavate the Meroe and El-Kurru Pyramids was to be on an expedition that would document its findings worldwide. Because of this, Anand's rich father Timbuku made it his mission that he get a foreign F1 visa and be accepted at the University of Michigan in the study of Classical Archeology. He always wanted Anand to study in America and return one day to continue his grandfather's mission.

Anand opened his backpack and removed a leather binder full of research papers on the lost civilization of the Kush nation. Then his team satellite phone began ringing.

Anand smiled as he recognized the caller's number.

"Hi my love," he greeted in Arabic.

"*Are you okay*?"

"I'm fine Nafy…we're heading to the site now."

"*You be careful. The locals don't like white foreigners interfering in our history*."

"That's why they accepted me on the expedition."

"*I love you*."

"I love you too and don't worry," said Anand while looking at a picture of a Kush pyramid. "I'll be alright."

Meroe Pyramids

"*Just get back to Khartoum on time*."

"A month is a long time, and I will be there to marry you and your dad's money."

"*Maybe…you should marry him*."

"Nafy, you know he's too ugly." Anand then picked up a picture of his dad when he was a boy.

"*I have to go,*" said Nafy with the cell-phone away from her mouth. *"Mama's calling me. I love you…bye*."

"I love you too." Anand ended the call and stared at other pyramid pictures as he began to remember the story his dad told him.

Timbuku

1956

Anand's father Timbuku was nine years old in 1956 and forced to work on a small farm that grew corn and some wheat in Dongola Sudan which was north of the city of Al Dabbah. One cloudless day, he suddenly stopped walking as his sandals began to slowly sink in the dry hot desert sand. He was tired with a confused look on his face as he stared across the Nile River at a distant boat slowly sailing southbound. *I have had a fucked up life.* He thought in Arabic while wiping the sweat from his forehead. *Four years in this hot ass sun and not getting paid is monkey shit.*

"Timu come on!" yelled his friend Suni. "We have to fill the buckets!"

"No!" yelled Timbuku.

The boys were kidnapped from their hometowns by a former militia fighter who later had permission to keep them from the newly formed Sudanese government,

"I quit!" yelled Timbuku thinking about his grandpa and his stories.

"What…you can't quit," said Suni. "If you do, your father will lose his herd of goats."

"I don't believe that lie anymore." Timbuku then turned and walked toward the corn field that lead to the servants mud houses.

"I'm stealing a camel and going home," said Timbuku. Suni dropped the two buckets of water and also decided to quit.

"Can I go with you…to your village?"

"Sure, you're the blackest Egyptian I've ever seen and definitely will pass as a Kushite."

"A what?"

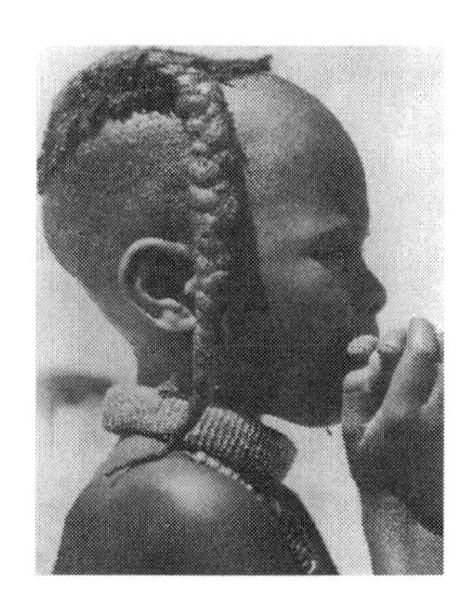

"A Sudanese."

"Oh," said Suni a little confused. "We have to hurry before that asshole comes looking for us after the midday prayers."

The boys began to run through the corn field, both smiling at each other knowing they would soon be free. Timbuku gathered food and water like a medieval pillager as Suni pulled the ex-militia's personal camel to the housing area.

The whole village was almost empty as everyone had already left for the mosque, for the (Dhuhr) twelve o'clock prayers.

Timbuku began to remember the first day he was taken away from his family as an indentured servant. He recalled his mother and sister crying as he was forcefully being pulled away by the wrist, by an armed stranger. “I don’t remember crying,” he whispered to himself.

The boys filled both sides of the tribal saddle bag with supplies, jumped on the camel, and rode from the village without being seen. Twenty minutes had past when Timbuku jumped off the animal as Suni stared. “What are you doing?”

“I am finding the way to Al Dabbah.”

“Are you crazy?” shouted Suni. “A leaf will not tell you the way to that city.”

“Be quiet and watch,” said Timbuku. “I saw a Bedouin camel trader do this before entering the desert.” He then placed a dented metal cup he pulled from the saddle bag on the hot sand and filled it with water. Then he took a leaf that floated and dropped it in the water.

“I hope you’re not wasting that water?” stated Suni. Timbuku then placed a sewing needle on the middle of the leaf and it began to slowly spin on top of the water and then stop.

"That way is north so we're going southeast," pointed Timbuku as Suni jumped off the camel.

"How do you know that is north?" asked Suni as he kneeled in front of the cup. "The other end of that needle could be north." Both boys were silent for three seconds.

"We are going that way," said Timbuku who stood up. "And you better hope I'm right or we're going to die in this desert."

"We have a fifty-fifty chance," said Suni, then drinking the water.

Three days later, after finding a main road and following it south, the boys were unexplainably exhausted and rode the camel into the town of Al Dabbah. There Timbuku asked for directions from a toothless local merchant on how to get to his hometown of Atbara. He told him either by train or by boat. They both decided to sell the camel because it had lost a lot of weight and smelled worse than the previous day. They hoped the sick animal would get them enough money to take the train to Atbara. They didn't trust the men that sailed on the Nile because of the killings and man-on-man raping stories their ex-militia owner told them.

After selling the camel to a fast food restaurant called *The Golden Humps*.

The boys found a cleaner reputable restaurant and ate out of a single bowl of beef and lentil soup with two spoons. When Timbuku took the last spoonful, he told Suni he urgently had to take a shit. He walked to the back of the restaurant as his stomach began to gargle like boiling water. He knew the soup was about to leak out his ass and saw his toilet, a single palm tree in the distance. Then a smell of rotting flesh hit his nose. In the back of the restaurant, he saw layers of fly infested meat hanging in an open steel cabinet as a thin man had just cut the head off a dead camel. *I knew that meat wasn't beef.* He thought while dropping his pants. He then held onto his knees and grunted in pain like a little dick Chinese man getting circumcised.

After fire-hosing the palm tree with his ass fertilizer, Timbuku and Suni walked for about an hour in the direction of the train station and were exhausted. Suni kept farting as he trailed behind Timbuku who walked at a quicker pace on purpose. They both felt as if someone was following them as they stopped to watch the red hot sun slowly sink behind the distant farms and desert that surrounded the city. It was soothing to everybody as the temperature dropped slightly every evening. The boys decided to rest in an alley behind a grain storage warehouse and sat along a cool mud brick wall.

"Timu…do you feel as if someone is following us?"

"I do, and there is no one."

"Tell me a different story your grandfather told you?" asked Suni.

"Okay…this one I believe is a true. Grandpa said at the time of British rule when he was eleven years old, he helped a great holy leader named Muhammad Ahmad temporarily chase the British out of the city of Khartoum. The white governor at the time was General Charles Gordon. His home and office including everything belonging to the British were looted.

Later my grandfather was personally given an Egyptian wooden box from Muhammad

Ahmad for his services in resupplying ammo to the revolutionary soldiers. The contents of the box were priceless jewelry and stolen by Egyptian tomb robbers who sold them to the General.

"Why didn't they just give him cash?" asked Suni.

"I don't know…just shut up. The box contained a gold Scarab (beetle) necklace, the actual earrings that Queen Nefertiti wore, and a stone….a replica of a larger stone that belong to the brother of the first black pharaoh of Egypt."

"There were no black pharaohs in Egypt," Suni said with conviction.

"There was…his name was King Piye."

"Was his first name meat or fruit?"

"Do you want me to finish the story?"

"Go ahead."

"Grandpa was told that the stone replica was the key to opening the hidden *Gates of Shabaka*." Timbuku then stood up. "Shabaka was King Piye's brother and Taharqa's uncle."

"Where are the *Gates of Shabaka*?" asked Suni.

"I don't know…stop asking questions. He also told me that a tablet was carved during the time period of the Middle Kingdom and it would reveal a secret."

"Your grandpa was high on hashish (marijuana)," said Suni while closing his eyes to sleep. "I have a hard tablet breaker in the Middle Kingdom of my pants and it's hanging right over my nuts."

"Don't ask me to tell you anymore stories," angrily said Timbuku as he sat down.

"I won't." Timbuku then leaned his head back and closed his eye while thinking.

“I believe we have enough money to ride the train to Atbara and then my mother will feed us until we burst.”

“I think I’m going to like your mother,” said Suni, opening one eye. “I miss my family.”

“Me too.”

The next morning both boys awakened a little agitated. “What is that smell?” asked Timbuku. “Did you fuck that camel?”

“No…and you smell like ass and hay,” said Suni while holding his nose.

“We both smell like the camel,” said Timbuku while waving his sweaty arms in the air. “I don’t remember sleeping on it in the desert.”

They both stood up, left the alley, and walked three more blocks. As they crossed the street, they both realized a man with a beard in his late thirties was following them.

“I think that man back there is going to rob us,” whispered Timbuku. “And then rape you.”

“No…you,” said Suni. “Let’s lose him behind that building then split up and meet at the train station." The boys walked quickly while peeking back at the pursuer.

"Run!" yelled Timbuku. They both ran down another alley between two buildings and suddenly turned in opposite directions. Suni could hear the man's running footsteps catching up to him. Timbuku knew the station was near as he heard a train-whistle blow in the distance.

"Suni…Suni is that you?" yelled the man as Timbuku glanced back.

"Don't stop Suni…that man doesn't know you."

"Suni, I'm your uncle," he shouted. "We've been looking for you for months. Your mother Mediza misses you."

"Mother," whispered Suni as he slowed to a stop. "Uncle Ackbar?"

"Yes, it's me!" Suni turned around and ran to his uncle with open arms. Timbuku kept running, not trusting the man and reached the train tracks that lead to the station. He knew Suni wasn't coming and would have to travel alone.

An hour later, Timbuku did not have enough money and had to beg the conductor to let him ride on top of the live chicken and grain storage compartment. He told a fake story of how his sister was raped and he was taken from his family and forced to work on a camel farm, shoveling shit every day. That's why he smelled like camel ass.

Chapter 2

Grandpa

The train traveled at a steady speed as the passengers watched the sun go down behind the never ending sand dunes. Timbuku got off in Atbara, never wanting to see or hear another live chicken in his life.

After purchasing a bottle of Coke Cola from a dusty machine, he walked slowly to the back of the station. It was completely dark outside and he knew it was too dangerous to walk alone. He decided to sleep close to a tall bright light post and wait till morning. *I miss my friend.* He thought curling up in the fetal position with the glass bottle of Coke Cola he couldn't open.

The next morning Timbuku was awakened by a gust of wind that blew sand into his face. He sat up in the morning daylight unable to see anything as the glare blinded him. He reached for his Coke Cola bottle and became angry. It was empty with a metal bottle-cap opener on the ground next to it. "Son-of-a-goat fucker," he whispered. "That was my breakfast."

He stood up and placed the opener in his pocket. Then he looked both ways and began walking southeast in the direction of the Atbara River.

Timbuku walked down the same long hill close to the river he remembered that lead to the mud house his father built. He began to smile seeing smoke rising from the back of low growing palm trees. He quickened his steps and then noticed someone exiting from the back.

"Mother!" he yelled. Shara looked up and her mouth fell open. She dropped the round flat tray made out of papyrus and ran to Timbuku. Her head scarf fell off around her neck as she kneeled and hugged him tightly.

"Hareek…Mubia!" she yelled. "Timbuku is back. God has answered my prayers." His father Hareek exited the house with an angry look on his face as his sister Mubia ran from the cooking fire on the opposite side of the house. They all gathered around ignoring his smell and hugged him.

"Where's Grandpa?" asked Timbuku.

"He's in the house," said Hareek. "He can't walk." They all escorted Timbuku into the house when his mother slowly awakened his grandfather.

"Daddy," Shara said softly as Grandpa Zula opened his eyes. "Timbuku is back." He tried to sit up while noticing how tall he got.

"Get your black ass over here and give your old grandpa a hug." Timbuku ran over and hugged him joyfully with closed eyes.

"Boy, you smell like zebra shit."

"I stole a camel and escaped."

"Did you fuck it?"

"Daddy, that's not a nice thing to say," said Shara.

"Son, you were to stay in Dongola two more years," Hareek said sternly. "And then come home."

"I hated it."

"We had no choice, but to let you go," said his mother. Timbuku then looked up at his father.

"That kidnapper beat us and lied that you would lose all the goats and Abigars (cows) if we didn't work." Hareek looked away in shame. "Why did you let him take me?"

"He was going to shoot us all if we didn't let you go," said his older sister Mubia who was getting married.

"Hareek…sell one of the maa'ez (goats) and send him somewhere safe," suggested Shara.

"Let's get the boy cleaned up and fed," said Hareek. "Then we'll talk."

"Grandpa, I brought you a gift." Timbuku reached into his pocket and gave him the bottle opener.

"Thank you son," said his grandfather. "My birthday was three months ago and nobody got me a present."

"Dad that's not true, we brought you your favorite dish from the city," said Shara. "Don't you remember?"

"That monkey ass stew was awful. I'd rather eaten that camel Timbuku fucked."

"Now you can buy sodas and open them," said Timbuku.

"You would think someone would invent an easier way to twist the metal tops off," said Grandpa Zula.

Fifteen minutes later, Timbuku ate a large bowl of butt burning *Salata Tomatim* (Sautéed tomatoes, green onions, and chili peppers.) for breakfast. He took a bath in the Atbara River and then sat with his family to discuss his predicament.

"Dad, I want to go back to Al Dabbah and find my friend Suni."

"Son, we decided you are to stay with your Aunt Dekunda," said Shara. "She will be glad to see you again."

They all knew the militia farmer was coming back to reclaim Timbuku so Hareek decided Shara would ride the train to Al Dabbah with him and find his friend Suni. Then they were going to Khartoum to stay with his aunt and uncle. Timbuku was happy.

Twenty minutes later, Hareek left the house for the train station to purchase two tickets. He didn't want to use the wedding money he saved up so he traded a cow for Timbuku's freedom. He received three tickets on the next train that was leaving early in the evening.

Meanwhile Timbuku sat next to his grandfather's bed and told him Suni loved his stories.

"Son, I need you to do something that is important for the whole country."

"What grandpa?"

"Do you remember the story about the square stone?"

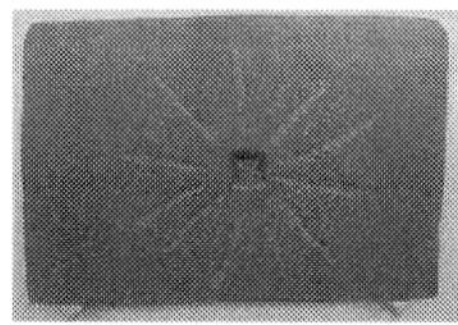

"Yes, Shabaka's Stone."

"When you get older," he said reaching for the famous wooden box. "I need you to find Shabaka's secret tomb that may hold the missing body of King Piye. It is said to be close to his pyramid, but no one has found it." Take this small replica of the stone with you and look for a door or wall that fits the indentation and turn it."

"I thought the tomb was already found?"

"That was the decoy tomb. Tomb robbers never found any gold which was always buried with Nubian kings."

"What will happen when I turn the stone?"

"I don't know. It may be a door that leads to the missing king or it may kill you."

"Kill me!"

Church of Our Lady Mary of Zion

"I once visited the patriarch of a Christian Orthodox Church in Axum Ethiopia who claimed his people guarded the Arch of the Covenant. So-called Black Israelites of America knew he was lying, but he did revealed to me that King Piye's son Shabaka built the Temple of Ptah that was surrounded by a great wall and gate. In that temple was believed to hold treasures, artifacts, including the Shabaka stone, and a stele of King Piye's location."

"What's a stele?"

"It's hieroglyphic recorded victories carved on slabs of granite. The patriarch told me that

Shabaka later secretly inscribed a clue on one of his steles. Only two steles were actually found and one was broken into three pieces."

"Let me guess Grandpa…I have to learn how to read hieroglyphics?"

"Yes, and find the broken stones. It may contain the location of the hidden tomb and King Piye's mummy."

"Where are the broken stones?"

"I only know…one is at the Museum of Cairo," said his grandpa while handing him the wooden box. "I never made it that far north, but this year Sudan is a free nation that's ruling itself."

"When did that happen?"

"In January."

"What month is this?"

"I think July," said his grandfather before coughing. "I don't have much time on this world so I am giving this quest to you."

"I will do my best Grandpa," said Timbuku while giving him a hug.

"You still smell like zebra shit."

The next morning Timbuku said goodbye to only his sister and grandfather. He left in tears, knowing it may be the last time he see's his grandfather alive. His mother carried a worn suitcase full of old clothes, the wooden box, and a prayer rug.

They reached the train station and were shocked to see through a fence, a mob of people fighting to get on the train.

"Run Timbuku!" yelled his mother. "We have to get on that train!" They ran and then turned in their tickets to board the train. Shara then grabbed Timbuku's hand and pulled him to the last cattle car that was partially full. They were helped on and managed to squeeze in with the passengers, mostly men that hung from the door. Some stowaways were jumping on the roof of the train as its speed increased.

"Mother, why are so many people on this train?"

"There are many job openings that were once filled by British citizens in Khartoum."

"I thought this train is going to Al Dabbah?"

"I'm sorry son, but we're going to Khartoum. We can't afford to stop and your dad will be sending money for you to go to school."

"But my friend is somewhere in Al Dabbah," said Timbuku as they both made it further into the crowded train compartment.

"When your father visits…he will take you to Al Dabbah." Timbuku began to sulk knowing he will never see his friend again.

"I promised your grandfather I would make sure you learned to read hieroglyphs in order to complete his mission your father didn't want to do."

"I know mother…you are right," said Timbuku hugging and squeezing her by the waist. "I love trains but not this one. My friend Suni said in America their trains have beds in them and servants that bring you food."

"Those beds are only for white people of America and the servants are descendants of slaves," said Shara.

"Are they still slaves mother?" asked Timbuku.

"No, they are paid for their services, but in small amounts."

"I was paid with bread and water."

"Your father heard that a rich man in America named Rockefeller paid a porter after he carried his bags ten cents. He threw the dime over his shoulder for the porter to pick up off the ground. His wife was so embarrassed, she reached into her purse and handed the servant a dollar." (True incident)

"What's cents and dollars?"

"Ten cents is seven pence and one dollar is about a British Pound."

"Oh."

"Your uncle will be so glad to see you," said his mother, changing the subject.

"So will Aunt Dekunda and her mustache," sarcastically said Timbuku.

"That wasn't nice."

"Her kisses feel like cat whiskers."

"She's had a problem with facial hair all of her life."

"Have you seen her chin?" asked Timbuku. "It looks like grandpa's hairy back."

"She is still your aunt and you need to respect her."

After taking a nap while standing up, Timbuku was awakened to the sound of all the passengers cheering loud with joy.

"Papi, I mean Mommi, what's going on?"

"You remembered your father's middle name."

It was asshole for a while. Thought Timbuku. *For letting that man take me away.*

"Khartoum has officially been made the capital of Sudan thanks to the P.D.P.

(Peoples Democratic Party) that formed a new coalition government."

"What's that mean?"

"More jobs and a brighter future for our people." Timbuku didn't believe her as he remembered the stories his grandpa told him of how other countries including Egypt constantly invaded Sudan in the past.

Khartoum Sudan 1956

It was late at night when the train pulled into the station in Khartoum as the passengers roared with cheers again. Shara and Timbuku jumped off into the darkness and ran with smiles. They were tired from the long ride and Shara knew exactly where to go. She had a return train ticket to Atbara and enough money to rent a room for two nights at the same motel she stayed in during her honeymoon. It only brought back memories of happy times before she had kids.

When they reached the motel, one room was available and they were both happy. In the room, Shara let Timbuku take a bath for the first time in his life. Then she tore and tied grandpa's old shirt and pants for Timbuku to wear.

"Put these on when you finish," she said as Timbuku slightly cracked the bathroom door open. Then he placed the clothes on the towel rack.

"Thank you mother." Timbuku then ran and jumped into the tub as the hot water caused him to pee uncontrollably. "Ouch!" he shouted as the clear water turn grey with a tint of yellow.

"Clean yourself and get out quickly," she shouted. "I know a place where we can eat."

"I could stay in here for hours," said Timbuku as he closed his eyes and then dipped his head under the dirty pissy water.

"What?"

"I'm washing my ass," he whispered.

"I can't hear you and I only have enough money for one meal."

"Can we split a burger?" Timbuku asked loudly from the tub.

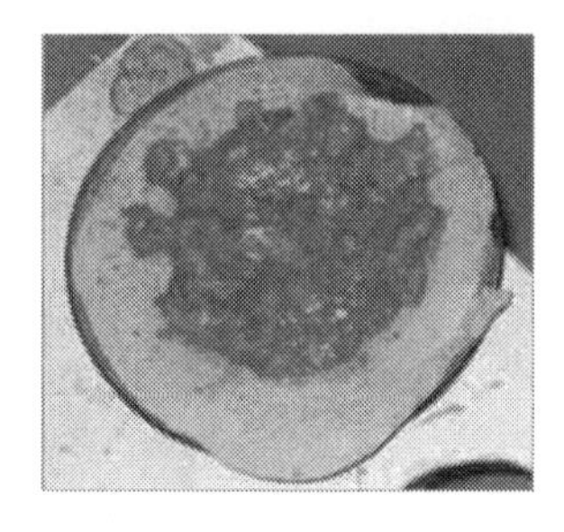

"We're not eating a burger," said Shara. "We're having Goraasa served with Tamia at the restaurant across the street." (Cube steak smothered in a garlic tomato sauce over sesame seed covered bread cakes.)

"Those cubes aren't steak," shouted Timbuku.

"How do you know it isn't steak?"

"Me and Suni discovered the secret as to why it taste so good."

"Why?"

"It's camel meat that's hung out to dry."

"No it isn't."

"Go to the back of the restaurant and look for a large box with small holes in it."

"You stay here…I'll be right back."

"I'm staying in the tub." *My ass crack has never been this clean.* Thought Timbuku. *And itch free.*

The next morning Shara and Timbuku walked from the motel with the suitcase in the direction of her brother's apartment that was south of the city.

"I will never eat Goraasa ever again," said Shara.

"Momma…that burger we ate last night," said Timbuku then pausing with a smile. "Wasn't cow."

"Are you shitten me?" she asked while stopping. "Tell me it wasn't camel?"

"Do you want me to lie?"

"It *was* tasty," said Shara while recalling the delicious flavor.

It was a little past seven in the morning when the recorded *Adhan* (Islamic call to pray) began to bellow from the top of a single mosque tower. Shara stopped, opened her suitcase, and unrolled her Musalla (Egyptian Prayer Rug). She then turned toward the mosque and handed Timbuku the rug. "Son, do you remember the Salaat (Islamic prayer from the Quran)?"

"I do."

"We will pray on that clean wood over there, northeast towards Mecca," she ordered while pointing at a building being constructed. "Timbuku didn't have the heart to tell his mother that he had converted to Christianity. Suni told him all the stories about Jesus and how he gave his life for all of us. Timbuku believed him because he blamed Islam as to why his prayers weren't being answered, to deliver him from slavery.

He bowed on the rug and silently prayed to Jesus and God as his mother smiled each time her head touched the wood. Timbuku didn't know why she was smiling, but was determine to ask her later.

After prayer, they finally reached Shara's brother's apartment. Timbuku loudly knocked hard and didn't stop until he heard his aunt screaming like a man with throat cancer from a back room.

"Hold your sheep's tail…I'm coming," shouted Dekunda. The door violently swung open and Timbuku's mouth opened. Dekunda's dark black hair was red on one side and her face looked like the hanging hairy testicles of the camel he sold. "Shara and Timbuku!" she deeply shouted. She then reached down and gave Timbuku a kiss on the cheek. He could smell the fumes of a cigarette as her five-o'clock shadow scraped across his face.

My aunt is a fucking chain-smoking hairy she-male. Thought Timbuku as Shara just waved knowing they didn't like each other.

"It is good to see my favorite nephew again…come in," she said while holding the door open. "Your lazy brother left to look for a job and will be back later." They all sat in the living room as a cigarette burned on an ash tray. "What brings you two to Khartoum?"

"Timbuku escaped from his government sanctioned slave owner and I am pleading that you let him live here?" Shara knew she couldn't have kids. "He needs to go to school at the request of my father and later restore honor to our family name." Dekunda smirked while taking a puff of her cigarette.

"Now that Sudan is a free nation," said Timbuku. "I can go to Egypt one day and visit the museum."

"You must first go to school and learn to read," said Shara. "If you let him stay, his dad promises to send money each month for his room and board." Dekunda then smiled.

"My husband will love for him to stay with us." Shara then handed Timbuku the box and his grandfather's old clothes that were in the suitcase.

Abizz returned home later that day as Shara and Dekunda cleaned and prepared a room for Timbuku. Shara talked to her brother for an hour about old times and then began to leave.

"Study hard and stay out of trouble," Shara said while hugging Timbuku. "I will bring your sister to see you in a month."

"Where are you going?" he asked.

"I am returning home, your grandfather is sick. Be brave and study hard."

"Yes mother." She hugged him tightly again and then turned to leave.

"Wait!" yelled Timbuku.

"What's wrong Son?"

"When we were praying on the wood…why were you smiling?"

"I remembered when I was a little girl, your grandfather and I was praying at a crowded old mosque. The floor was wooden and weak, and when your grandfather kneeled down, the wood cracked at the same time he farted."

"That is funny."

"He tried to explain that the noise was from the wood cracking, but the smell gave him away." Shara hugged and kissed Timbuku again, then left. She returned to the same hotel room. Two hours later, after making a few phone calls, she was visited by her first ex-husband.

The next morning, Shara's brother Abizz walked her to the station and she rode the train all the way back to Atbara with no panties on and a refreshing smile on her face.

2010

Anand put his father's picture back in the leather binder after recalling the story he was told when he was ten years old. The Range Rover trucks had just stopped at the site and the local helpers were already unloading tent poles and ropes from the top of their van.

Chapter 3

Golden Ankh

The base camp tents were set up in record time as the expedition team started unpacking equipment. Anand shared a tent with a young American archaeologist named Brian. They had two cushioned cots, a table, one chair, and hot sand under an old rug for a floor. Brian had just walked in with a case of bottled water as Anand opened his backpack. He didn't unpack and was excited knowing he would be close to solving a part of his great grandfather's lifelong quest. He opened an old map written in the Sudanese language (Arabic) with an underground diagram of all the pyramids in El Kurru.

"I hope we find rare artifacts that will substantiate the timeline of Nubian affiliation with Egyptian culture?" stated Brian. "Dr.

Ember has evidence that artifacts are buried here in Meroe."

"Did he tell you that?" asked Anand.

"I overheard him mention it on the phone at the airport."

"He was just buttering up the people who financed this expedition," said Anand. "King Piye was buried at El Kurru. I think we'll find maybe a broken vase here or some worthless artifacts that will be added to the museum in Khartoum."

"When did you get so negative?" asked Brian.

"I just don't want to waste my time here. I told Dr. Ember that El Kurru has untouched pyramids that are buried in layers of desert sand."

"And how do you know this?"

"Because I am Sudanese," said Anand while holding up his maps. "And my grandfather's notes may lead us to one of them."

"If we don't find anything in two days, I will suggest to Dr. Ember that El Kurru might be more successful." Anand then looked down at his maps.

"Tell him to dig directly behind all the pyramids."

"Why?"

"According to my records," lied Anand. "The servants were buried close, to serve the kings in the afterlife."

"I will tell Dr. Ember." Brian left the tent as Anand opened his leather binder again that revealed a picture he took at a Berlin museum. He then began daydreaming as to how he took the picture and acquired a valuable artifact.

It was a year ago (2009) when he flew to Germany to continue his mission thanks to his dad Timbuku. He booked an Egyptian exhibit tour online to the Neues Museum in Berlin. The tour guide was a female named Rosewitha. She was the ugliest pale white woman he had ever seen. There were eleven visitors on the tour that was being partially renovated that morning and Anand smiled and stared at her, to let her know he was interested.

"And this here is the beautiful single eye sculpture of Nefertiti," tour-guide Rosewitha said in English with a German accent. "We don't know why her eye is missing, but some scientist believed she really had only one eye." Anand then raised his hand.

"Where was this artifact found?" he asked while smiling and then winking at her.

"That is a good question. It was found in Amarna Egypt by a German archaeological team, led by Ludwig Borchardt in 1912." She then smiled at Anand and he knew she took the bait.

After the tour of half the Egyptian exhibit, Anand stayed behind and asked the tour guide to dinner.

Later that night after consuming two more beers and a glass of wine at her apartment, he later was in bed with Rosewitha with the lights out. It wasn't dark enough because he could still see her face and offset teeth. He humped her hard as he stared at the head board while trying not to throw-up. She screamed like a flying witch that just got splintered from her broom.

"That was delicious she said while breathing heavily." Anand then pulled out while still hovering over her.

"You were amazing too," Anand said looking away as if she was Medusa. "I would've really liked to see the renovated section of your museum? I'm doing my thesis on Egyptian hieroglyphics."

"The museum is closed on Thursday. I can show you around then."

"Really!"

"It's not a problem, now kiss and stick me one more time," she demanded.

God, please blind me like Stevie Wonder. Thought Anand as he put on another condom over the one he had on. "Open those sexy legs" *You ugly bitch.* He knew he had to take one for the team and shoved his face into hers. She stuck her tongue deep into his mouth and he farted. It was a shock reflex, the same as if a man was being held at gun point. Except he almost shit in the bed.

Two days later, Rosewitha met Anand at the museum as contractors were installing more security cameras throughout the museum. She earlier paid a security guard to let them in the closed off renovated section at the back of the building.

"I want to take a lot of pictures of hieroglyphs," said Anand. "To translate them on paper."

"I can read some," said Rosewitha. "The most interesting writings…are on the pictures of Tutankhamen's tomb."

"Let's start with the tablets on the wall," said Anand. "Then work our way to the tomb behind the caution tape."

They both walked into the closed off exhibit area where numerous artifacts were displayed in glass cases all along the middle of the floor.

Rosewitha began talking and smiling as if she was giving a tour. Ignoring her, Anand looked to his left and saw what he was looking for. He quickly walked over to the broken stele with hieroglyphics. He took a picture and then stood with his mouth slightly open. *This is Shabaka's third broken piece.* He thought. *It connects to the ones in England and the Egyptian Museum in Cairo.*

Then he remembered the partial translation he couldn't decipher on the other two broken pieces until now.

Amun will shine his blessings over the King, the Queen, and *his children.* And eternal life will forever be *entombed in the Altar* ***until he victoriously returns from the North.***

"Entombed in the Altar," read Anand as a look of curiosity and disbelief fell upon his face. "Oh shit. This is a prophecy," he whispered.

"What's wrong?" asked Roswitha. He then remembered on the previous tour that a chipped tablet was incased in glass in the next hall. Anand walked quickly past the caution tape as Rosewitha followed. He reached the tablet called the *House Altar*.

House Altar (Shrine)

It was a two layered limestone with a carved picture of Akhenaten, Nefertiti, and three kids sitting under the rays of what looked like a sun. He read the hieroglyphs above Nefertiti's head. *In this, the blessings of Aten will open the doors from eternal rest.*

Anand knew what he was about to do could land him in prison, but curiosity took over his rational thinking. He took a picture and then kicked the tall case over, breaking the glass as the tablet fell onto the museum floor.

"What the fuck are you doing?" yelled Rosewitha. She then ran to get a security guard. Anand flipped over the tablet and took another picture of the faint hieroglyphs on the back. He then picked the tablet up and ran to a secluded corner of the museum. After making sure he was not in view of any security cameras and contractors, he slammed the tablet to the ground. A solid gold Ankh, the symbol for eternal life, fell out the middle of the broken stones.

Roswitha walked quickly towards Anand as a guard followed behind and saw him put the gold Ankh in his backpack. It was heavy and the size of a cell phone. Anand ran out the closest emergency exit door like a Kenyan marathon runner. The guard and Roswitha exited the door fifteen seconds later and Anand was nowhere to be seen. She knew she had just lost her job.

Anand hid the golden Ankh well, before reaching the airport twenty minutes later. He flew an expensive one-way flight back to Sudan without incident. He knew Rosewitha was going to get in trouble, but didn't care. She was a casualty of war, a piece in his quest that helped him solve a puzzle. That key he held up his ass in a large zip-lock bag was going to help him find the lost mummy of King Piankhi. Anand's father Timbuku later discovered that the small replica of the Shabaka stone was not a key, but a souvenir from the British Museum in London that held the original. It was used by a farmer as a millstone wheel to grind grain into flour. (True)

Shabaka Stone

The real key was up Anand's ass and he knew he had to concentrate on the meaning and all the pharaohs that were affiliated with it. It was like starting over for him, but he knew he was pointed in the right direction.

During his first class flight from Berlin, he noticed on the picture he took of the *House Altar* (Shrine) fourteen rays of lines with four Ankhs on lines one, two, seventeen, and eighteen.

House Altar (Shrine)

Those kids have elongated skulls and their dad is wearing a dress. Anand began smiling as the plane hit some turbulence. *And what are those appendages extending from their ankles?* His irrational thoughts began to make sense while looking at the Altar. *Those Egyptians pharaohs must be fucking aliens and there has to be three more ankhs out there somewhere.*

Chapter 4

El Kurru

Anand blinked steadily as he ended his recollection daydream while putting the picture back in his leather binder. Then he looked up, seeing Dr. Ember's only geologist Tom, enter his tent.

"Dr. Ember wants to see your maps of the pyramids."

Anand then bent over in pain while holding his stomach. He then moaned in extreme agony. "Get help!" he yelled.

Four minutes later his tent was filled with expedition team members including Dr. Embers. They determined Anand had appendicitis and needed to get him to a hospital. He was placed in the backseat of one of the Range Rovers with all his belongings including a satellite phone and driven by a local helper toward the town of Shendi.

The hired help drove like a drunk driver toward the main road when Anand sat up.

"Keep driving south to Khartoum," he said in Arabic. "I'll pay you for your troubles if you keep quiet." The driver nodded yes as Anand opened his wallet and paid him the equivalent of a hundred dollars. He smiled throughout the whole trip. *I need to go to El Kurru first and then the Valley of the Kings*. Thought Anand knowing Akhenaten tomb was found but not Nefertiti's. *There has to be a clue there that relates to the golden Ankh.*

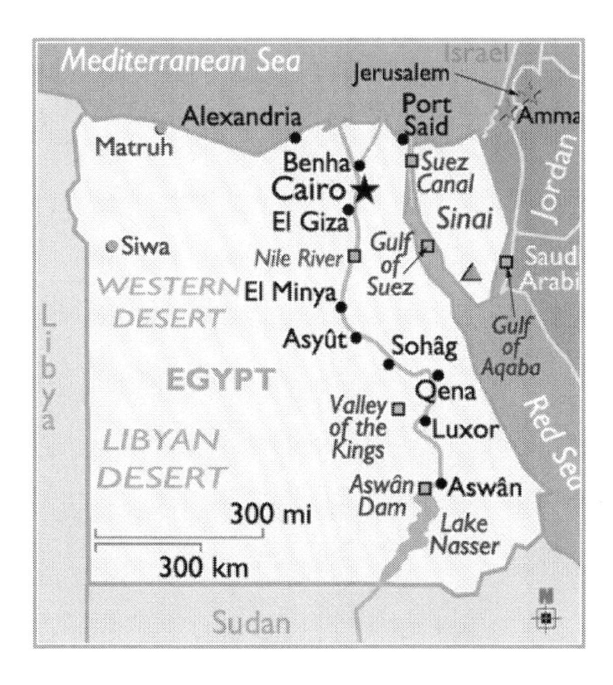

Anand reached Khartoum knowing his authorization expedition documents were still good and hired three more workers to help him at El Kurru. He later borrowed with a renter's fee, a newly acquired *Ground Penetrating Radar* from the National Sudan Museum. He believed he knew where to dig at King Piyes pyramid thanks to his father Timbuku's research papers.

1971

Timbuku was 25 years old when he left his crying wife and two young boys in Khartoum. It was his second time visiting the El Kurru Pyramids and he wanted to test a theory. He needed to investigate the top of the intact pyramid of King Shabaka. It was believed by local elders that the pyramid was just a solid one piece shape, but he believed there was much more hidden.

At the top of the pyramid was thought to be an air vent hole, but actually was a star viewing chamber. Each pyramid in Giza Egypt had a dead end chamber below the entire structure. Timbuku knew the dead end chamber was used for loading large objects.

All Sudanese archeologists knew that King Piankhi's Pyramid had two horses buried in the chamber with a decoy mummy. Nobody knew how they got in there or what happened to them. Timbuku climbed up with a rope to the top of Shabaka's pyramid, dug away layers of sand from the vent hole, and discovered indentations in the bricks. He believed something was placed there at an angle and probably stolen by the Assyrians who destroyed most of the other pyramids.

Later that afternoon when the sun slightly set on the vent side of all the pyramids, Timbuku climbed Shabaka's Pyramid again and used a mirror to reflect the sun's rays down into the vent hole. There were piles of sand that blocked a collapsed back entrance to the outside and Timbuku knew that might be how King Piankhi's mummified horses were carried in.

The next morning, he had his two hired-helpers dig away the sand from behind Shabaka's tomb. They hit a partially collapsed tunnel that lead to the main burial chamber. Timbuku entered alone and stumbled on a secondary wall under the pyramid. He began reading faded hieroglyphs that he hoped would reveal a clue. *The rays of Horus will bless our king as his journey to Orion will not be alone. Queen Galhata will...* "I can't read this shit," he whispered while moving more sand away. Then the back wall began to crumble as a square solid gold reflective plate fell with the sand and rubble that poured into the collapsed tunnel. *This probably was used to reflect starlight into the chamber according to the hieroglyphs.* Thought Timbuku while covering the dusty gold plate with his beige multi-pocketed archaeological vest.

Then he climbed from the collapsed tunnel and walked directly past his helpers toward his truck.

Two months later, Timbuku sold the gold reflective plate to a museum curator from the Charlottenburg Palace in Berlin Germany. In the palace garden, the newly rebuilt tea house that was destroyed in World War II was topped off with a solid gold basket with three kid-like statues holding it up. Timbuku knew it was his gold that was melted down and placed on top of that building.

The newly formed *National Museum of Sudan* couldn't prove, but were told by his helpers that Timbuku removed something heavy from the tomb of King Shabaka. It didn't help that he was a wealthy man overnight and because of that, he was banned from visiting all the Kush Pyramids, especially King Piankhi's. He didn't care but knew he had to pass on his research to his two son's Anand and Kintu. He knew something that no other archaeologist in the world knew, that the Kushites knew how to read the stars.

****

2010

Anand and his four helpers, thanks to having excavation documents provided by Dr. Embers, were allowed to pass a fenced-off police checkpoint before reaching the El Kurru Pyramids. They stopped directly in front of King Piankhi's pyramid and set up a tent.

The entrance was closed off as he noticed the pyramid had eroded due to the passing of time. Anand decided to call his dad and ask him to translate the notes he couldn't read on page five about the pyramid. He dialed his expedition satellite phone and waited for a connection.

"Father, can you hear me?" he asked as his signal was weak.

"It's your mother."

"Hi Momma, I need to talk to Dad. Is he still not feeling well?"

"He's still grumpy as usual. Wait a minute, I'll hand him the phone." Anand heard walking and then coughing.

"Who is this?" asked Timbuku in Arabic.

"It's your son, Anand."

"Why do I smell monkey shit?"

"Papa, I'm at the pyramid of King Piye and need to know what you meant about a tunnel or wall on page five?"

"No…I smell zebra shit." Timbuku then realized he was reliving the day he returned to Atbara when his grandfather asked if he was fucking zebras.

"Papa, listen, did you find part of a broken tunnel or wall near King Piyes pyramid? I can't read your handwriting on this page."

"Son, the mind is a terrible thing. I can smell the day I escaped from slavery."

"Papa, are you going to answer my question?"

"I already did." Anand became frustrated.

"I found a key and it has something to do with Nefertiti."

"Did you say fur on titties?"

"No Nefertiti," shouted Anand. "Did you visit her tomb?"

"I sure did and took pictures. The *Valley of the Kings* is the most important find in Egyptian history." Timbuku then paused in silence. "Did you know those crowns vibrated?"

"Put Momma back on the phone."

"Fuck you too," said Timbuku.

"I'm sorry son, your dad's on medication that's affecting his mind. Yesterday I was his sister Mubia. Today…I'm his maid and he keeps demanding I give him a sponge bath."

"I gotta go," Anand said hurriedly. "You take care of yourself and him. I should be home tonight."

"You stay safe Son," said his mother with concern.

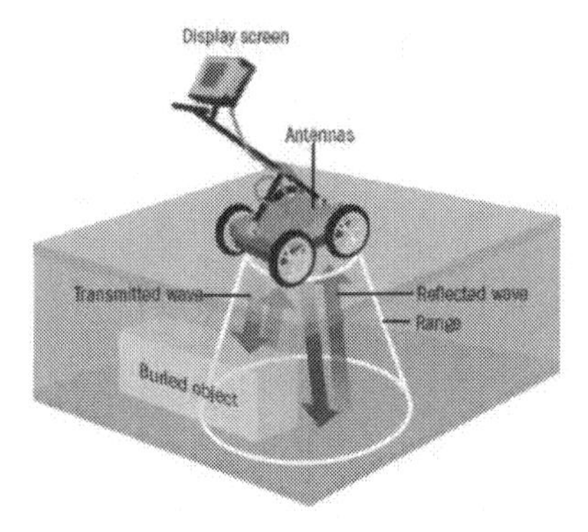

Anand then walked to the back of the pyramid and began operating a new *Ground Penetrating Radar*, the first one ever used in his country. It didn't indicate anything as he continued walking backwards and then sideways. He was about fifty meters behind King Piankhi's Pyramid when he spotted square shaped cuts of lime stone that resembled a tunnel. He then place four stakes indicating where to dig. Anand believed he found a damaged unlooted chamber of King Piankhi and knew nothing significant was there. He set up halogen night lights and gave the men till morning to reach the chamber. They were offered one hundred dollars each if they could complete the task before sunrise. The men were digging like escaping twenty-five-years-to-life prisoners and the last juicy pussy in the world was at the bottom. Anand knew the one gay worker imagined a hard dick was down there.

Before sunrise, the men reached the chamber ceiling that connected to a long tunnel. It was caved in completely, in a downward slope. Sand had destroyed most of the chamber including a large box of broken bottles that contained unrecognizable food and possibly water. It also contained jars of organs that were removed from King Piankhi and his wife Queen Abar. The chamber was only a symbolic vessel to feed the king and queen in their afterlife.

Anand called the National Museum of Sudan and asked them to send out an excavation team. He then decided to have the same helper that drove him from the Meroe expedition, return Dr. Ember's truck and the satellite phone he didn't answer after he picked up a rental car in Khartoum. Then he was going to drive to the *Valley of the Kings*.

Chapter 5

Nafy

Anand rented a dusty blue Chevy Suburban in Khartoum and then drove to his fiancés house first. Before he could get out of the rental car Nafy had already ran from the house.

She jumped into his arms, ignoring the laws for displays of public affection as Anand believed she gained ten pounds (four kilograms). “I missed you so much,” she said while kissing his salty unwashed face.

“I’ve missed you too, but you know how important it is for me to complete what my father started.”

“Remember, one month then we’re getting married and going to New York.”

“Nafy, can we go somewhere else? The white people in that city are rude and the blacks are dangerous…like the Iraqis.”

"I've been to Bagdad and the people there are courteous and friendly."

"I'm talking about the American soldiers there," Anand said in high tone. "Even though they knew, they kicked my ass because I looked like Osama Bin Laden."

"You do look like a young Bin Laden with no beard," said Nafy while rubbing his face. "I still want to go to America."

"I think my visa may be cancelled."

"Why."

"I broke and stole a valuable artifact from Germany."

"I wondered why strange men with foreign badges were here looking for you."

"What did they say?"

"They wanted to know where you were and I told them you were out of the country…in London."

"What nationality were they?"

"One looked Ethiopian, but I think the others were Jordanian." Anand became worried.

"I have to go Nafy."

"Why?"

"The artifact I stole is putting you in danger. I have to get rid of it and then we can get married."

"You come back here in one piece." Anand kissed her deeply and then rushed back to his rented Chevy Suburban.

"There was a man with a badge that walked with a limp," shouted Nafy. Anand started the engine and drove toward home when Kintu called him on his cell phone.

"Anand, Dad is getting worst."

"I'm on the way to the house now."

"I should be there shortly," said Kintu. "I'm on the highway."

Timbuku's health had been slowly deteriorating for about a month. He was coughing more frequently and a doctor was called to the house. When Anand arrived, he ran through the mini-mansion he grew up in and into his father's room.

"Mother, what's wrong?"

"Your dad has pneumonia."

"How bad is it?"

"The doctor doesn't know, he called for an ambulance and they said two hours is the earliest they can get here."

"Tell them he's white and British," angrily said Anand. "They'll be here in ten minutes." He then walked to his father's bedside, kneeled down, and held his hand.

"Son, it is good to see you. Did you complete the mission?"

"Yes father. I found King Piye's hidden tomb and it was filled with old life giving treasures."

"Boy, I know you're talking about those canopic jars full of organs." Anand then slowly reached into his pocket and handed him the golden Ankh. A single tear fell down Timbuku's face as a smile cracked. 'Son, thank you for almost completing the family mission. This is mentioned in King Piye's stele and it will find his mummy."

"The National Museum of Sudan is collecting the treasures as we speak."

"Our king will be home soon…and tell your brother he sucks…for not helping you."

"He's married and has to take care of his kids."

"I forgot," coughed Timbuku. "You still smell like hairy gorilla testicles."

"I thought it was zebra shit?" smiled Anand.

"That too…and send my maid in here. I need my nuts scratched."

"Dad, that's Mom…not the maid."

"I know who she is," said Timbuku then coughing again. "She fired my sexy maid last month and I planned on driving her crazy."

"She thinks *you are* crazy."

An hour later, Timbuku was taken to Fedail Hospital and later diagnosed to having about a week to live. Anand, his mother, and Kintu's wife followed the ambulance to the hospital and waited to be allowed to see him.

When they reached his hospital room Timbuku was partially awake with oxygen breathing tubes up his nose. His eyes were closed as the beeping of a heart monitor was at a slow steady beep. They all walked in quietly and Timbuku opened his eyes slowly.

"Where's Kintu?" he asked.

"Dad, he will be here soon," said Anand.

"Who?" asked Timbuku, forgetting that quickly.

"My husband," said his wife. Then the room door swung open and Kintu walked in. He kneeled at his father's bedside as the oxygen air tubes in his nose began sounding like Darth Vader.

"Father it's me, Kintu." Timbuku smiled and then frowned as he turned his head toward him.

"Where the fuck have you been? That maid has been worried sick about you."

"I want you to meet someone."

"It better be President Obama," said Timbuku who then laughed and coughed. An old man entered the room and Timbuku tried to sit up. Tears began to run down his face as he recognized who it was. "Suni, is that really you?"

"Yes, it is me…Timu."

"Get over here and give me a hug…you old black camel fucker."

"Father, I've been looking for him for years," said Kintu. "And with a little help, I found him at the Port of Sudan."

"What have you been doing all these years?" asked Timbuku while wiping his eyes with a tissue.

"After we escaped, my mother hid me from that militia slave pimp for a few months and later we moved further north. That's when my uncle taught me how to build boats."

"Didn't that kidnapper tell you to stay away from those man-on-man raping boats?"

"Those murder stories he told us were lies just to keep us from escaping."

"It has been so long," said Timbuku as he began to weep. "I looked for you in Atbara after my mother and sister were killed in the house fire."

"It was my uncle who decided that we all should move further up the Nile River. We built boats close to the border and sold them to wealthy Sudanese that fished on Lake Nassar."

The family all left the hospital room as the two men shared stories about their adventures in Sudan. Kintu had driven night and day to transport Suni to see his father.

Two hours had past when the two men said their goodbyes. The next day, Timbuku's health turned for the worst. He slipped into an unforeseen coma as his wife held his hand for three hours before he died. His family was sad, but glad he died peacefully.

Following Islamic tradition, Kintu and Anand washed his body and then placed it in a cotton shroud. Even though Timbuku was a closet Christian, he was buried at the Khartoum Common Wealth War Cemetery. He illegally paid for a special burial plot next to his Grandfather Zula who fought in the East Africa Campaign.

At the beginning of that war in the summer of 1940, Italy invaded Sudan and Timbuku's Grandfather Zula joined the Sudan Defense Force. Fierce battles were fought and the

Italians were later defeated in January of 1941.(True) After the war, Grandpa Zula told Timbuku he was on a convoy that guarded the Meroe pyramids. It was said that the Egyptians secretly paid the Italians to flatten all the pyramids. (Not True)

During the burial, Anand asked Kintu for a favor and he agreed. A day later, he returned the rental car and flew to Egypt to complete the new mission he was on. He had to find out what Nefertiti and the golden Ankh had to do with the victory stele (historical tablet) of King Piankhi.

It was said in history books that no one knew where Nefertiti came from. Anand was determined to find out by visiting the *Valley of the Kings* and the Cairo Museum. He believed the Egyptians were hiding something historical they didn't want anybody to know about.

Chapter 6

Port Said

"Has my package arrived?" asked Anand on his hotel room phone. There was a moment of silence. "I'll be right down to get it." He slammed the phone receiver down as anger filled his heart. *These stupid ass Egyptians need to stop speaking English*. He put his backpack on and ran three flights down the emergency stairwell. He didn't trust the elevator that squealed like a constipated soccer player getting kicked in the nuts. After signing, he grabbed the box from the front desk and took it into the lobby rest room. In the farthest stall he opened the box, smiled, and then dialed his cell phone. "Thank you big brother…this may save my life."

"*I had to pay a lot of cash for that thing*," said Kintu on the phone.

"I will give you your money back when I return."

"*You be careful in Egypt*," said Kintu with concern. "*The news is saying they are on the brink of a revolution, maybe even civil war*."

"I have to take a long bus ride to the *Valley of the Kings* and then I'll drive out of this shitty country."

"*Where are you now?*"

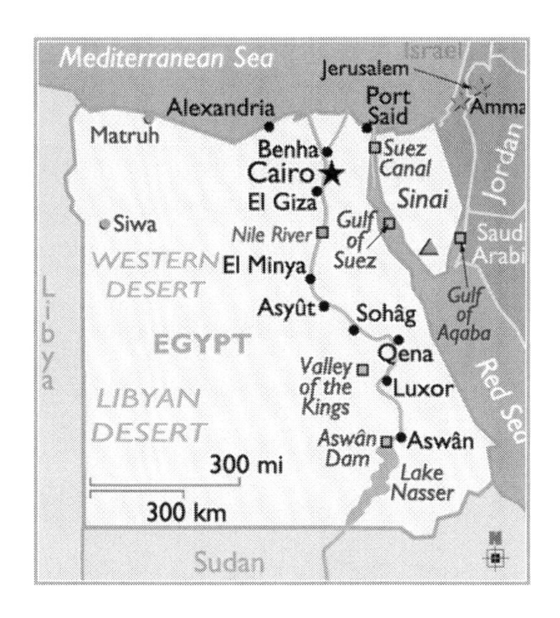

"In Port Said, at the only hotel in Sinai Egypt with an available room."

"*Call me when you leave so I know you're not being ass raped by Egyptian radicals who believe in government change and free love with men and women.*"

"I always knew you were a closet homo. I'm stealing your wife and going to fuck her like the camel humpers of Yemen."

"*If you touch my wife…I will cut your balls off and sauté them in olive oil.*"

"I hope you're not going to eat them?"

"*Shut up and get out of that country.*"

"I will…cannibal."

Anand left the hotel with his backpack full of research papers. He waited patiently along the sidewalk for his bus to arrive. Anand had paid two touring companies to take him to the Cairo Museum and then to the *Valley of the Kings*.

Then a shiny black BMW quickly drove up and stopped in front of him. An Ethiopian man in a black polyester suit jumped out as another came up from nowhere and grabbed his back-pack. They pushed Anand into the backseat of the car and threw his backpack into the trunk. The driver slammed the car door as the other Egyptian man jumped in next to him. The tour bus was just arriving when they sped off.

Anand was afraid and wondered if he would be dead in a sand ditch by the end of the day. Suddenly the tour bus exploded and the car shook as the rear window cracked from the shock wave.

"You guys saved my life," said Anand in Arabic while looking back.

"We know," said the angry looking driver. "The bus was government sponsored with Korean foreigners on it."

"Why did you save me?"

"We didn't save you," said the Egyptian next to him. "We were ordered to kidnap you."

"Where are we going?"

"Just shut up and enjoy the ride," shouted the Ethiopian driver.

The car drove for three hours and arrived at a large mansion in Alexandria Egypt. Anand sat still as the back door was opened by the driver who noticed a look of relief on his face.

"You black Sudanese dog," angrily said the driver. Anand had pissed his pants like a four year old and just smiled.

"Get your nasty ass out of my car," shouted the Egyptian next to him. Anand stood up out the car as piss ran down his leg. The men pushed him toward the servants side door entrance as the driver whispered into his cell phone. The three then took an elevator to the third floor of the mansion as a Filipino maid placed a clear sheet of plastic material across a plush white carpet. The large open area had one office desk along a back wall and a painting of a white Egyptian princess behind it. The men pushed Anand onto the center of the plastic. He knew for sure he was going to be shot or chopped up into many pieces.

"Get on your knees…you fucking freak," said the Ethiopian driver as he kicked Anand in the back of his leg. A big belly bearded Egyptian in a black suit with a red tie exited a door as a toilet flushed. He then sat at his desk and relit a half smoked Cuban cigar.

"Mr. Anand Abbul, do you know who that woman is in the painting?"

"Is it your wife?"

"I wished…that hippo never looked that good. It is the last pharaoh of Egypt…*Queen Cleopatra."*

"I always thought she was black?" Anand was then smacked in the back of the head.

"Being an American educated Sudanese, you know the history of how she seduced Julius Caesar and Mark Antony."

"She was the lover to both men who liked to dip in a little chocolate," said Anand. "Later committing suicide."

"Dip in what?"

"English slang for interracial sex."

"She only used Julius Caesar…to keep the Romans from taking over Egypt. In history it is told that Caesar was murdered by a group of his own senators. But in fact…it was Cleopatra who began the killing." The fat man then took two puffs of the cigar, coughed, and then cleared his throat. "Our secret Egyptian history tells us she stabbed him in the back after threatening to take her off the throne. The senators found Caesar wounded and knew it was their chance to finish him off. She then left Rome knowing Mark Antony would later send for her."

"What does this history lesson have to do with me?"

"You have something I want and if I don't get it…I'm going to have you stabbed."

"I don't have any Viagra." The smiling driver behind him pulled a hidden knife from between his butt cheeks.

"I want the golden Ankh you stole in Germany."

"I don't have anything gold." The Ethiopian driver then stabbed Anand in the arm, just above the elbow. He fell over in pain holding his arm as blood dripped onto the plastic.

"If I don't like what I hear next…he's going to stab you in the kidney like Cleopatra. Do you understand me Julius?"

"Oh yeah…I do have the golden Ankh," said Anand while continuing to hold his bloody arm. "It's in my hotel room." The fat man looked up at the driver's partner.

"He opened the box on the toilet and I checked his hotel room thoroughly including his backpack."

"Okay," shouted Anand. "Okay…don't stab me again."

"Where is it?"

"Up my ass."

"Stab him in the stomach."

"No…it really *is* up my ass." Anand then farted and it sounded like a kid's balloon losing air.

"Pull it out of him."

The men yanked Anand's pants down as he was forced to lay on his stomach across the plastic. The Ethiopian driver with the big hands reached deep down into his underwear and between his ass cheeks. Anand screamed like Michael Jackson in *Thriller* as he reached into what felt like his colon and pulled the Ankh out forcefully. Excrement and blood oozed out and he felt like Mike Tyson after his boxing promoter raped him, financially.

"Clean it first and bring it to me," excitingly said the fat cigar smoking man as the hand raping driver followed the maid into the kitchen. "I thank you and Egypt thanks you Mr. Abbul. Roll his shitty ass up in the plastic and take him out the back entrance."

Anand was carried down three flights of fire-escape stairs and then thrown into the trunk of the same car. He knew he was probably going to get shot and tossed into the open desert. After a half-an-hour had past and with considerable effort, Anand unrolled himself from the plastic.

That was fun. Anand thought in pain. *In one day, I've pissed on myself, got stabbed in the arm, and shitted in my underwear after being fist fucked by an Ethiopian knuckle dragging gorilla.* "Egypt sucks," he whispered. *I need a vacation, somewhere safe, maybe Baltimore or Ferguson Missouri.*

(Those cities had nation-wide media coverage where the police killed unarmed so-called African Americans.) True

Mostly in large cities all over the United States so-called unarmed blacks and some whites are killed by cops that claim they feared for their lives. Almost all cases, the police officers are never charged with murder. (TRUE)

Chapter 7

Valley of the Kings

The car finally stopped and Anand was ready. He was in position with his back-pack on when he heard the car key go in. It was completely dark outside when the trunk slightly opened and then he pushed it up at full force. The trunk hit the driver in the nose as he painfully fell backwards. Anand then jumped out the trunk and ran into the darkness like a Kardashian that was offered a marriage proposal from a white man. The other Egyptian rushed to help his friend off the ground.

The car had stopped at a shipyard as Anand saw and smelled three docked garbage barges. The bloody nose Egyptian sluggishly stood up, pulled out a pistol, and blindly fired three shots. Anand never looked back as he ran toward some dim lights of an office building. *Those bastards were going to throw me in the trash.* He thought while thanking God they didn't steal his wallet filled with cash and credit cards.

Anand knew he had to get a ride, but smelled like piss and shit. He entered another building that processed the delivery of garbage trucks and asked to use their restroom. He then took off his pants, underwear, and washed them in the sink. He knew that peeing on himself may have save his life including shoving that golden Ankh up his ass. He tied his underwear tightly around the stab wound and put his wet pants back on.

After walking for two hours Anand finally found an unoccupied taxi that drove him to the Cairo University hospital.

They stitched and bandaged his stab wound for forty eight pounds ($75.00 US dollars). He took another cab and paid for the long ride back to his hotel room.

In his hotel room, Anand painfully undressed with one arm and sat in the tub for thirty minutes. He soaked his torn anus while thinking about that fat Egyptian and how he knew about the golden Ankh. Anand's mind kept drifting back toward that ugly German bitch he fucked. He believed she had connections with that Egyptian mob and snitched. He got out of the tub, dried off, and then dialed his cell. "Brother, I was right…that bitch in Germany had me followed. I was almost killed tonight."

"*Did you give it to them*?"

"Not really…they pulled it out my ass."

"*I told you since we were kids to stop hiding things up there*."

"I know."

"*The toys you hid were smaller than that thing*."

"I now know what a prisoner feels like after a full body cavity search."

"*Get your smuggling ass crack back to Sudan*."

"Not yet…I'm renting a car and then going to the *Valley of the Kings*."

"*Why*?"

"When I first flew home from Germany with the Ankh, I x-rayed it at the Sudan Museum and discovered some kind of ancient electrical circuit is embedded in it."

"*What do you think it is*?"

"I believe it's a key to a door or a secret tomb…hopefully with King Piye's mummy and his treasures."

"*I hope you're wrong because when those Egyptians find out that gold plated Ankh I had made is fake…they're going to hunt you down.*"

"I hid the real one in the ceiling vent of the lobby restroom," said Anand while adjusting the bandage over his stab wound. "Hopefully this cursed thing will be out of my hands when I return to Sudan."

"Call me when you're across the border."

"I will."

The next morning after retrieving the real golden Ankh, Anand walked out of the hotel as if he had rode a horse for forty days. His ass was still throbbing as he rubbed his bloody bandaged. He struggled to raise his arm for a taxi as one stopped. He jumped in and the driver started his overpriced meter.

"Let me guess?" asked the taxi driver in broken English. "You need…ride to hospital."

"No…to a car rental."

"That bloody bandage looks pretty good…I mean bad," said the cab driver.

"It'll be alright. I was stabbed by robbers."

"I just want you to know…that not all Egyptians are bad. It's only a few that are ruining the tourist business."

"That bus bombing yesterday didn't help," said Anand.

"This is only temporary," said the taxi driver while glancing back. "Egypt is changing and everybody's talking about a revolution. You're safe…being an African American, but other tourist may want to leave this country soon."

"I am Sudanese." The cab driver then began speaking in Arabic.

"The people of Egypt are organizing a government takeover. Next year in 2011, we will all unite against President Mubarak."

"Why next year?"

"In secret…people are spreading the word to save up supplies, money, food, ammo. The country will be at a standstill and we will force the government to hear our demands."

"You do know the government may crack down…like in China."

"The will of the people is strong and like Obama said in 2008. We say…change will come to Egypt."

"A lot of people don't like the changes Obama has done to America…especially the Affordable Care Act."

"Our greedy government is slowly getting rid of free health care," said the cab driver.

"And more and more people are dying especially the children."

"Sudan is a long way from having a viable health plan that works."

"What does *viable* mean?" asked the cab driver.

"Successfully works."

"My third wife told me…I am not viable in bed so I'm divorcing her."

"I am so sorry to hear that."

"My brother is *viablinging* her every week and she doesn't know I know." Anand smiled. "I should have her stoned to death."

Then there was a moment of silence as the cab driver looked through his rear view mirror. "We are being followed. I think the government knows I've been spreading the message of revolution."

"No, they look like foreigners," said Anand while looking back. "They probably want me."

"Why?"

"I don't know exactly, but I have a good idea." Anand wanted to lie and tell him it was because of his ancestral Nubian kings that ruled his country in the 25th dynasty. "Can you lose them?" asked Anand.

"I sure can and get you to your destination in one piece." Anand buckled his seat belt and the cab driver transformed into an angry *Indy* race car driver. He turned down numerous roads and then sped down the main street as the following car was nowhere to be seen. He skidded to a neck-snapping stop in front of the *Hertz of Egypt* car rental office.

"Thanks and how much do I owe you."

"This ride is half price," said the cab driver while breathing heavily. "I haven't done that in a long time, since I cheated on my second wife with the third." Anand paid the cab fare and quickly rented a Toyota Land Cruiser with special tires that rode on desert sand. He had no intention of returning the vehicle in Egypt knowing more than one organization was after him.

Anand concentrated his thoughts on what to do next. He knew according to Dr. Ember, there were sixty five tombs discovered including the one that held the body of Nefertiti at the *Valley of the Kings*. He decided to continue his journey southwest for three more hours before reaching the VOK admissions gates. His cell phone began to vibrate as he was parking and it was Nafy.

"*Where are you*?"

"A hi honey or hello would be nice."

"*You haven't called me in since your dad's funeral and mother has stopped planning the wedding.*"

"I will be there soon. I am trying to complete my dad's mission."

"*I don't like it when you're in other countries. The Arabs are sometimes irrational and violent.*"

"I am safe and close to solving the mystery," lied Anand. "I have to go…I will call you tomorrow."

"*Do you promise*?"

"I will try," said Anand as he got out and locked the SUV door.

He noticed a bald man wearing a long black *thawb* staring at him. Then the man then turned and walked with a limp toward the entry gate with other tourist.

Anand walked casually after paying an entry fee and the Egyptian guards seem to ignore him. He was black like some of the locals and wasn't the nationality of the average traveling tourist. They didn't even warn him about taking pictures with commercial cameras including his cell phone.

Anand knew there were sixty five tombs discovered including the one believed to have held Nefertiti's mummy. The Egyptian government only reported sixty three and he only had to find the two that were so secret.

KV62 tomb

A half an hour later, Anand met up with a group of Americans and Japanese tourist that waited for the Egyptian tour guide to exit from the KV62, Tutankhaman's tomb. The guide had just finished with a group of overweight German tourist, mostly women. Anand knew Egypt first ruled Nubia during the New kingdom in which gold was mined and given as gifts. *That gold Ankh must've been made for Nefertiti or her husband King Akhenaten.* Anand thought to himself. He believed after his studies in college that Nefertiti and Akhenaten were brother and sister. He also knew, after remembering his photos, that Tutankhamen had deformities in his bone structure requiring him to use a cane to walk.

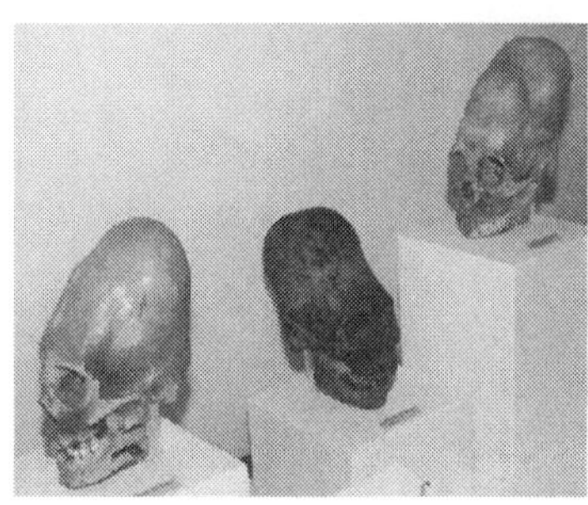

I wonder if Tutankhamen's skull is also elongated? Anand thought to himself as the tour guide reached the group. The overweight German women were sweating like NBA players during Aids test day. They smelled like bacon on top of molded cabbage as the group walked past him toward their tour bus.

Hitler would roll over in his grave if he saw those fat bitches that represented his country. Anand then remembered Roswitha in Berlin. *Ugly beats overweight any day. You can't put a paper bag over those double neck she-cows.*

The group then began their decent into KV62, toward Tutankhamen's tomb. The tour guide spat out gibberish bits of information as Anand kept his eyes open for any hieroglyphic clues.

Ten minutes later, Anand noticed a painting on the tomb wall of two people holding Ankhs. One he believed was Tutankhaman with a cane.

At the end of the tour, Anand also noticed that the mummy of Tutankhaman didn't have an elongated skull and was really black. *Blacker than Wesley Snipes*. He thought as all the tourist slowly exited the tomb. Anand then asked the Egyptian tour guide in Arabic, if he could take him personally to tomb KV35.

"I'm going to lunch," said the tour guide. "And the government has restricted tours to that tomb."

"Would one hundred American dollars be enough?"

"I don't need to eat…and for that amount, you can diddle my wife."

I don't fuck Egyptian whores. Thought Anand as he followed the smelly man out of the tomb and then to his government owned jeep. They drove west to KV35 and Anand knew that tomb was used as a graveyard in the Third Intermediate Period. Over eleven mummies were stored there and he believed another clue may present itself.

They walked and then descended into the tomb as a column of local workers were carrying numerous fake artifacts into various chambers. Because Anand was black, the men ignored him as the tour guide began to explain the history of King Amenhotep.

"Can you show me the secret ante-chamber of the three mummies that were discovered here in 1898?"

"It's just behind here," pointed the tour guide. "The British believe that one of the females is Nefertiti."

"Do you think it was her?" asked Anand.

"I'm not paid to think...but no. I believe Nefertiti was an alien."

"Why would you say that?"

The tour guide leaned closer to Anand. "Have you see the shape of her head and King Akhenaten?"

"I saw her kids."

"It's been rumored for centuries that they talked to each other only using their minds," whispered the tour guide.

"I heard the same thing," lied Anand.

"Last week," said the tour guide. "I saw two British men being escorted into tomb KV65 which was discovered in 2008. I believe something strange is going on down there."

"Can we visit it?" asked Anand in English.

"For fifty more dollars and only at night," said the greedy tour guide. "I heard the guard will do anything for money."

"Make it twenty five."

"Okay…but I have to pay the guard in advance to let us in. Meet me at the entrance gate at 9:00 pm."

"You better not stand me up or I'll report you to the museum," said Anand while opening his wallet.

"Why would I stand you up? Are you going to fall?" Anand then explained in Arabic after showing his papers that if he stood him up, he would get his dick massager cut off for stealing money from an American sponsored archeologist.

"I would never steal from you," the tour guide said in Arabic. "I need my hands to wipe my ass."

Anand had forgotten that most Arabs didn't use toilet paper and then remembered to never shake their left hands. (True)

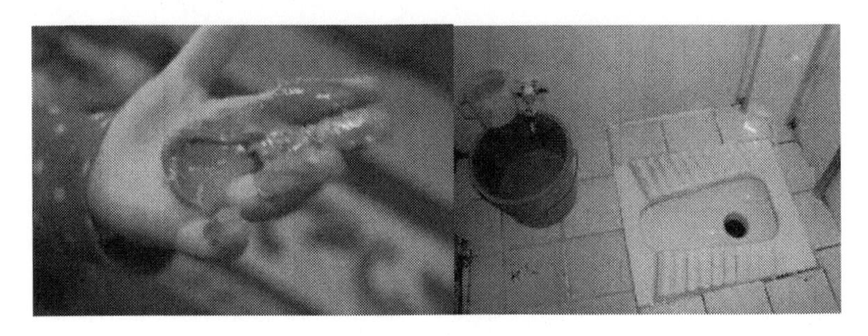

Chapter 8

The Crowns

It was 9:32 pm and a clear night when the under-paid guard opened the chain locked gate of KV-65. He only allowed Anand to enter the chamber because he didn't trust the tour guide. Anand figured out why. He didn't pay the guard all the money he promised.

Anand walked down the poorly lit entrance to the first chamber and noticed a gas generator with its exhaust pipe hooked to a long tube that exited through a drilled hole in the stone ceiling. He decided to start it and the whole tomb lit up like Yankee Stadium. He then walked in one chamber and notice expensive test equipment next to a wooden crate that was partially opened. It housed an ancient female sarcophagus. *This doesn't look that old.* He thought. *But damn heavy.*

Anand picked up a nearby pry-bar and broke open the rest of the crate. He encircled the limestone sarcophagus and stopped. He was amazed at a clue he found including a tag on the crate written in Arabic; *The Property of the Cairo Museum via Queen Alia International Airport, Jordan.* He looked closer at the bottom of the sarcophagus and saw a recessed indented black picture of the Ankh, a little smaller than the golden one he stole from Berlin.

He then took pictures of the sarcophagus with his cell phone before walking into the furthest chamber, not believing what his eyes witnessed again. There was a chair with wires connected to a round mechanism that held up what looked like the White Crown (Hedjet) worn by Egyptian pharaohs. *Maybe the tour guide was right.* Thought Anand as he was tempted to sit in the chair, but decided to look around some more.

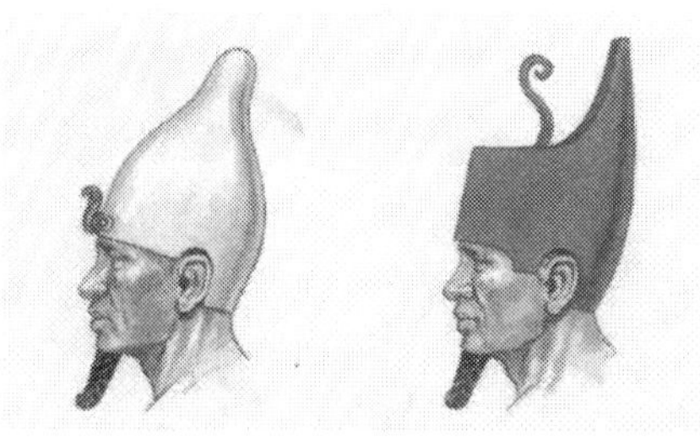

He noticed one Red pharaohs Crown (Deshret) with two more deteriorated white crowns next to a log book written in English.

How were these artifacts found and transported from Jordan. He asked himself while looking at small x- rays of all four crowns. They indicated an unknown electrical component that internally encircled each lining of the crowns. Anand almost forgot how hot it was in the tomb as he began reading the log book to himself while sitting in a nearby chair.

We successfully powered up crown 1A at 24 volts with no synaptic reaction according to Dr. Akbed. He checked into the Cairo Hospital as a precaution with no unusual symptoms. My colleague Dr Richards, with authorization from the Egyptian government, will conduct the test combining specimen 1A with 1B, hopefully tomorrow after we chisel open the limestone sarcophagus.

"Not if I can help it," Anand said out loud. He then set the power level on the electrical converter to 30 volts.

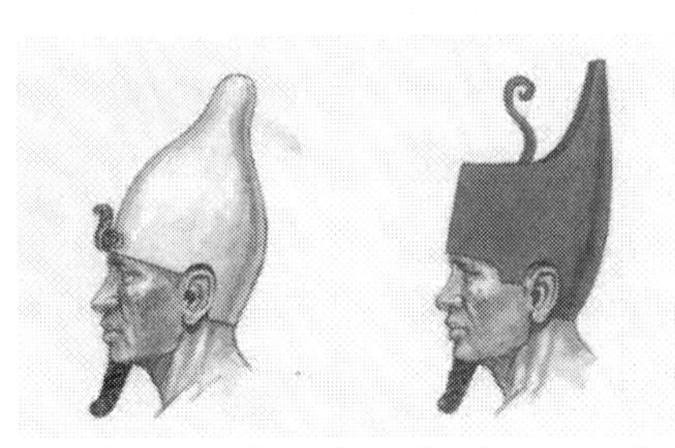

He sat in the wired chair and placed the White Crown on his head. Fear overtook his body, but he knew it had to be done. The crown began to hum from the surge of electricity and there was no reaction to his mind or body. He was hoping to maybe mentally see the universe or get a glimpse into the future. There was nothing as he sat and contemplated. *I don't want to do this but I must.* He then removed the white crown, shut off the converter, and walked over to the red one.

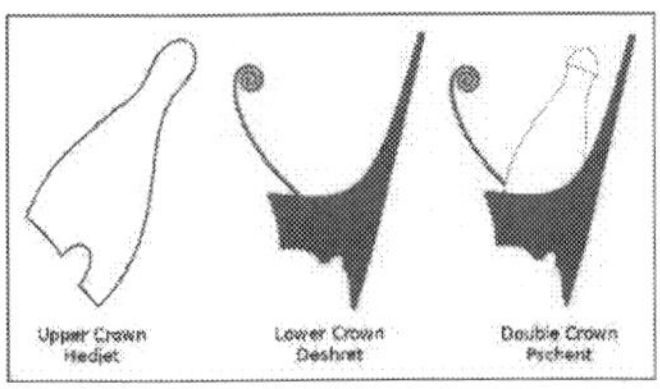

He combined the white crown with the red and turned the machine on again. Before he sat down, he pulled his cell phone from his pocket and made a video recording. "*In case I fry my brain or maybe die in this chair. I wish to leave this recording...that I am doing this for the Sudanese people and my father.*

And brother, I fucked your wife a month before you were married."

Anand was more afraid of his brother seeing the video as he placed his cell phone back into his pocket. He reached up and lowered the two crowns on his head. He just sat there as the vibration began to tickle his ears. For three minutes nothing happened as he began to believe it was only a head massager. *Maybe I need a weak mind to control.* He thought looking to the back of the chamber at a painting of a Persian soldier holding a Roman sword. *I know how these artifacts got to Jordan.* Anand remembered in history that the Neo-Assyrians pushed the Kush out of Egypt and destroyed all the temples and pyramids built by the Nubian kings. *These artifacts were looted and taken to Petra Jordan.* He now believed King Piankhi's treasure was looted by the Assyrians and possibly hidden somewhere in the Petra caves of Jordan. The Bedouins have been searching for buried treasures for hundreds of years in that sand buried city. (True)

I know the British are financing digs in Petra and hope to find something else not from this world. Thought Anand. *Nefertiti and Akhenaten are either real smart with cranial birth-defects or hybrids* (half human half alien).

Another minute had past and Anand decided he was wasting his time. *This thing doesn't work,"* he thought. "Wait a minute," he whispered while standing up. *They didn't have batteries back then. These hats may be solar powered.* He sat back down, turned his head toward the halogen lights, and waited two more minutes. There was nothing happening so he pulled the crowns from his head and stood up again. He opened the log book and took pictures of the first eleven pages. Anand return to the first chamber and shut the generator off.

When he reached the entrance of the tomb, the guard patted him down carefully before he jumped into the burping tour guide's jeep.

"What did you see down there?"

"It was nothing…three chambers, some paintings, tagged wooden artifacts, and a generator for lighting. I believe those men were just taking pictures."

"They did carry cameras a few times."

The tour guide drove Anand back to his rental car. He opened the hatch-back door of the Land Cruiser and pulled the hidden gold Ankh from under the spare tire.

After paying the main gate guard, Anand drove back to tomb KV-65. He then fake smiled as he walked toward the guard while waving. "I left my cell phone in one of the chambers," he said in Arabic. *You land stealing Assyrian refugee*. The guard then held his hand out for money.

"Ten pounds," said the malnourished guard as Anand opened his wallet. He knew it was the equivalent of 15 dollars and gave the guard a twenty dollar bill.

Assyrian Empire ruled from 900 to 607 BC. and over the years mixed with white Edomites and became a lighter complexion. (TRUE) Research Esau from Edom.

He quickly walked and reached the sarcophagus while pulling the golden Ankh from his back pocket. When he was about to place the Ankh onto the recessed indentation, he looked down and his dick suddenly became very hard. He was standing there with a porn-star boner that began to hurt. “I can’t believe this shit,” he whispered. *Those fucking hat’s were for those limp dick pharaohs*. He then smiled. *I couldn’t get it up either if I had to fuck my sister*. He then placed the Ankh on the sarcophagus while wanting to jerk off and nothing happened. *My dick is harder than an Egyptian obelisk.*

The sarcophagus suddenly began to shake as the eyes of the painted face began to glow white. Then the sarcophagus partially opened as a dim light began to flicker. Anand leaned down and peered with amazement as he noticed a naked body. “It’s Nefertiti,” he whispered in astonishment while looking at her hairy nappy pussy.

Nefertiti

She looked like she was buried yesterday as her beauty was truly…that of an *Ebony Magazine* super model. The Egyptian queen was only wearing the same crown like the sculpture in Berlin and a triangle shape string necklace that layed between her large areola breasts.

Anand tried to remove the crown from her head to check for elongation but it was stuck. He then took a picture with his cell phone and unsnapped the necklace from around her neck. The lid of the sarcophagus began to close as the flickering light went dead. Anand didn't notice he was standing too close and jumped back quickly. He paused in fear realizing the lid had almost closed on his hard horizontal pointing dick. He swore he noticed Nefertiti smile as he leaned down while looking in. Only one eye glowed on the closed sarcophagus lid as the stone's seams began to disappear. He quickly placed the triangle shaped necklace around his neck and held the gold Ankh like a weapon. *I'm going to have to fight that guard.* He thought looking down at his zipper. *I just hope he's not gay and grabs my dick.*

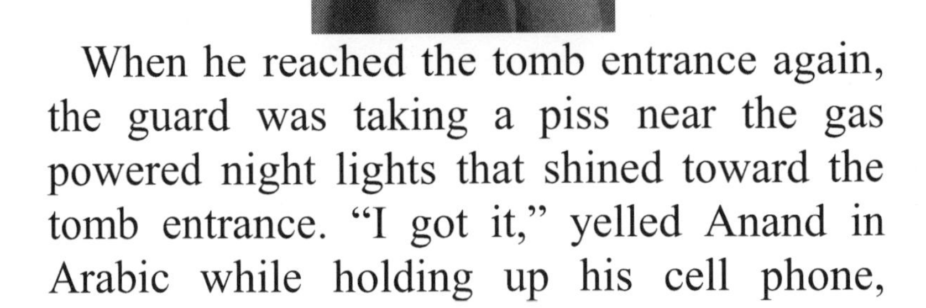

When he reached the tomb entrance again, the guard was taking a piss near the gas powered night lights that shined toward the tomb entrance. "I got it," yelled Anand in Arabic while holding up his cell phone, hoping he didn't notice his bulging pants. The guard waved for him to leave while still holding his willy with the other hand.

Anand got into his car and drove all the way back to the hotel with his dick almost touching his belly-button. *It has never stayed up this long.* He thought grabbing his back-pack and then sprinting into the hotel while covering his protrusion. He successfully reached his room unnoticed while dialing his brother on his cell phone. "Kintu!"

"*What's wrong little brother*?"

"I entered a secret tomb tonight and discovered the British actual found an upper and lower pharaoh's crown."

"*I want you to get out of that country. The British are more dangerous than the Egyptians.*"

"You're right, but my jink is hurting."

"*Did you catch another STD? I'm telling Nafy.*"

"No, it was the crowns. They're mind and body enhancing machines like Viagra…and I used one."

"*Leave now stupid,*" Kintu said urgently. "*Just stay away from border checkpoints. A man from International Customs called.*"

"For what?"

"*I don't know, but he had a German accent.*"

"I have to take a cold shower."

"*Don't get caught or you'll be getting a warm pissy one from a German prison guard.*"

"It's called a golden-shower and I can't leave Egypt, not yet."

"*Don't tell me why...just stay off the cell phone. They are probably tracking it.*"

"I will and you won't believe what else I have to tell you."

"*Just stay safe little brother.*" Anand hung up and then took a long cold shower until his wanker subsided. He got dressed, sat on the room bed, and picked up the triangle necklace. He placed it back around his neck, then searched his cell phone pictures of the hieroglyphs that were on Nefertiti's sarcophagus.

Chapter 9

Tutankhaman

Anand then read while whispering, "The sun god Aten will ascend the mistress of two lands to the shores in the north from which she came." He paused in thought and then remembered King Piankhi's son Taharqa had an ocean town in Spain named after him (Tarraco). (True)

"Could it be referring to the shores of Spain or even Alexandria?" he asked himself while packing and then leaving his hotel room six minutes later. He drove and found a secluded café down the street with Wi-Fi and signed onto his laptop. With half a hard-on, he researched again to refresh his memory of how the son of King Piankhi, Taharqa was known for saving Jerusalem in the bible from the Assyrians (2Kings 19:9 and Isaiah 37:9). (True)

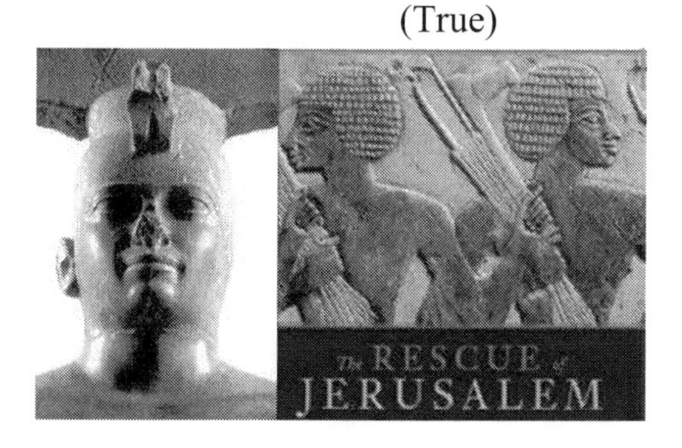

It says Taharqa and his army may have reached the Pillars of Hercules. Anand read to himself. (Rock of Gibraltar).

Rock of Gibraltar

While researching the meaning, he came across an image of the Debod Temple in Madrid Spain. He then searched for any pictures taken of hieroglyphs inside and out of that temple.

Debod Temple in Madrid

This temple was built by the Kushite King Tabrigo. Thought Anand. *Donated to Spain in 1968.* (True)

Abu Sibel was the location of the temple in southern Egypt and was in danger of being submerged in water because the Aswan Dam being built.

Anand then remembered Ramses II and Nefertiti's temples were also relocated to higher ground. He searched all the hieroglyphic photos of the temples and found nothing.

He leaned back in his chair at the café and paused. *Whoever hid that golden Ankh in the tablet I broke, knew it would open Nefertiti's sarcophagus.*

Almost an hour had passed as the sun was at high noon and Anand grew frustrated from searching online. He knew most temples were looted over the years and decided to give up. He was no more closer to finding King Piankhi's mummy than his grandfather. What he did know was his golden Ankh was a key used to open a sleep stasis sarcophagus for a gorgeous looking woman that ruled over the weak minds of Egyptians many years ago. *I have to notify the Sudanese government about the sarcophagus and the crowns before visiting Taharqa's Temple.* He thought. *Then I'm going home and selling the gold Ankh online.* He knew the original Taharqa Temple was in Kawa Sudan near the town of Dongola where his father Timbuku was enslaved before 1956.

Anand closed his laptop and packed it into his backpack. He then left the café and jumped into his rented Toyota Land Cruiser. He knew something was wrong when two tall Egyptian men sat up from hiding in the back seat.

"Where were your heads down there?" asked Anand looking in his rear view mirror. They didn't say a word as the front passenger door remotely unlocked and opened quickly. Anand recognized it was the bald man with the limp he saw at the *Valley of the Kings*.

"Drive," he said in English with a slight Arabic accent.

"Why are you following me?" nervously asked Anand.

"Do you have the key?"

"What key?"

"Don't play stupid, Mr. Abbul," said the Egyptian. "Do you have the *Symbol of Salvation*?"

"Are you're talking about the gold Ankh?" asked Anand in a nervous tone. "I sold it."

One of the silent men in the back seat began searching Anand's back-pack and handed the limping man the Ankh.

"Drive to the Giza Pyramids." Anand then felt a gun tap his shoulder.

"That Ankh is the property of the Sudanese government," said Anand as he began driving.

"We know you stole it from Berlin and it is rightfully ours," said the limping man as he waived a small black crystal over it.

"What does it open?" asked Anand, already knowing it was Nefertiti's sarcophagus.

"It will free my mother and help us return home."

"Is that somewhere near the constellation of Orion?" guessed Anand.

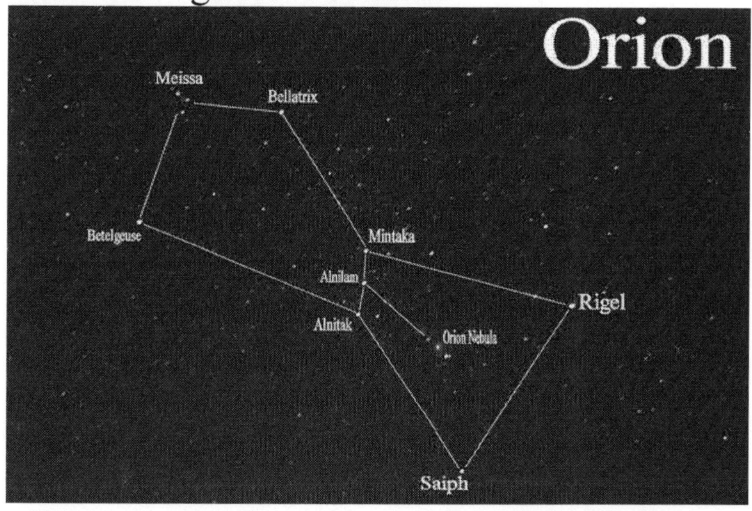

"Yes…near the star cluster of Alnitak?"

"I didn't study astronomy," said Anand. "But what I do know is…Nefertiti is definitely not from that star cluster. She is from here."

"Looks are deceiving Mr. Abbul."

"No way…she is fuckable."

"My father ruled these lands centuries ago, and you found one of four keys that will free my mother."

"How did you know I had the Ankh?"

"We purchased a fake one from an Egyptian in Alexandria. After getting our money back forcefully, his maid told us it was pulled from the rectum of an African man from Sudan." At that very moment Anand's ass began to hurt again.

"My fourth question is..." Anand hesitated to ask. "Are you Tutankhaman?"

"I am."

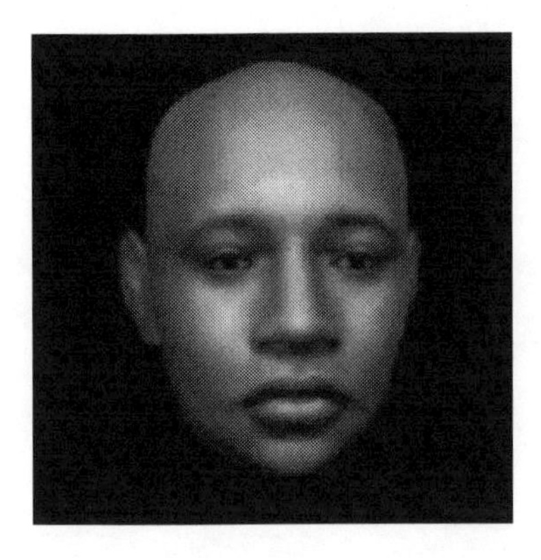

"Then who is that black as toast mummy in your tomb?"

"A Roman's love-child from a Nubian slave who suffered from osteoporosis."

Anand's mouth fell open for a second and then he asked. "If you are not from this world and highly advanced. How come you couldn't fix that fucked-up leg?"

"The medical practices of the Egyptians at the time of my birth were barbaric and my parents were stranded here when our ship had to suddenly leave on an emergency rescue mission."

"Do you mind telling me why?"

"A distress beacon on our *Pinir* midway station was activated. My father thought it was destroyed because our ship can't make it back without fuel and supplies from that station. The ship should have returned twenty years after they left." Anand's eye brows raised with curiosity. "Before I was born, my mother and father including their men were captured by the Nubians while retrieving high tech tools from King Piankhi's tomb.

"Don't you mean they were tomb robbing?" Anand said angrily.

"No, they never found the tools the Nubians stole from Egypt," said Tutankhaman. "They were unable to make it back to the ship on time and were presumed to be dead. That's what my father told me."

"What happened after they were capture?" asked Anand.

"My people including my mother and father were released unharmed and decided to separately return to Egypt. My father Akhenaten returned alone and used one of the ships R.S.S (Rejuvenation Stasis Sarcophagus) to bring recently dead animals back to life especially hawks.

This amazed the Egyptian priests who worship many deities including Horus, whom also resembled a hawk. They began to fear him and made him pharaoh because he had control over life and death. He later created a new one god religion called Aten, to control the weak minds of the people.

"What happened to Nefertiti?" asked Anand.

"My mother supervised the construction of a mobile safe haven up north. Years later she returned to Egypt and ruled by my father's side."

"What happened to his other wives?" asked Anand.

"That's not important," angrily replied Tutankhaman. "When the Persians were invading Egypt, my father hid Nefertiti's sarcophagus in KV-35 which kept her alive until we could moved her."

Yeah, so later he could fuck his sister again. Thought Anand. *And produce more crippled little fucks like you.*

"Earlier in time, when our ship was not repaired for space flight, our leader forced the Egyptians to build three larger pyramids around 2055 BC. They needed to harness power from the sun and send a message to our *Pinir* station that we were still alive and well."

"You do know P.N.R. when you drop the (I's) means *Point of No Return*?" asked Anand.

"No…I didn't."

"Many Egyptians believe the pyramids were built for the pharaohs," said Anand. "To live again in the afterlife."

"That is what we wanted them to believe," said Tutankhaman. "My father completed the modifications on the already built Khufu (Giza) Pyramid. The first two pyramids, Khafre and Menkaure act as generators that feed plasmatic energy into the main pyramid you call Giza. We unsuccessfully tested the rescue beacon that only shined brightly high in the sky one night around the time your *Hebrew Messiah* was born."

"Let me guess," said Anand. "The star of Bethlehem was actually your signal you tried to send into space?"

"Maybe."

"That's bull and camel shit," angrily responded Anand.

"My mother told me a long time ago," said Tutankhaman. "That our prophet *Rovas* walked with righteous wisdom on our world during the time your genetically inferior cousins still lived in caves."

Your momma's inferior. Thought Anand as the lunch traffic was getting heavy. "Rovas is actually "Savior" spelled backwards without the "I" and why are you taking me to Giza?"

"You are to be a witness," lied Tutankhaman.

"A witness to what?"

"We will let you know…if all goes well."

"I am no threat," pleaded Anand. "I just want to get back to my fiancée."

There was a frigid silence as they drove onto the main highway called Ring Road that lead to Giza. It took Anand thirty minutes to drive his silent captors to the pyramids.

As they reached the main tourist entrance, the guard recognized Tutankhaman and waved the rental car to pass as Anand grew more and more unsettled. His thoughts then became disturbing. *I wonder if these aliens have a taste for human flesh.* Anand then fake coughed. *I'll keep hinting that I'm sick and tell them, I have Sickle Cell and Aids mixed with a scorching case of Herpes.*

Tutankhaman ordered him to stop the vehicle in front of the *Khufu Ship Museum* which was right next to the Giza Pyramid.

Khufu Ship Museum

All the men got out as the two seven foot three giants followed behind Anand. They entered the museum and walked toward the plank that hung at the center of the ship. The men walked onboard the delicate ship as Tutankhaman turned back toward Anand.

"Do you know how old this ship is?"

"I've read in my studies that the solar barge was built in the 4th dynasty," said Anand. "Around 2600 BC." (True)

"Actually 2680 BC. King Khufu (Cheop) is said to have travel down the Nile in this very same boat and was the first pharaoh to introduce Egyptian culture to the Nubians."

"I haven't read anything that would substantiate that claim…in Egypt or Sudan."

"This is why we need the key," said Tutankhaman. "To unlock our proven historical records." He walked into the dark compartment room and placed the golden Ankh on the middle of the floor. The room began to glow yellow and then a door on the floor of the ship began to open. Tutankhaman stepped back with the Ankh and a large sarcophagus slowly rose up from a lower inner chamber. He then placed the golden Ankh on the side of the sarcophagus and the painted eyes began to glow. The lid then opened as a woman began to suddenly come to life.

She is fucking ugly. Thought Anand as the naked female sat up.

"Mr. Abbul…meet my mother Nefertiti."

"That's not Nefertiti," pointed Anand. "Nefertiti is a woman of great beauty and her face is recognized all around the world."

"That woman you are referring to is my father's third wife. Her name is Kiya."

"Are you telling me history is wrong?"

"It was the only way to keep my mother alive when the Persians conquered Egypt."

"Kiya is in KV-65," said Anand.

"Are you sure?"

"Yes, she looks like the Nefertiti we all know."

"We will go and revive her."

"You better hurry because the British are going to crack that sarcophagus open like a Hamas farmer behind a virgin goat."

"We may need your help in moving it out of the chamber."

"Are you crazy…that thing weighs a ton."

"We have tools to move heavy objects."

"I knew the ancient locals had hi-tech help in building the pyramids," whispered Anand.

"Follow me," ordered Tutankhaman. "My mother won't be able to walk for about an hour."

"If I slept on my back for 1300 years…I don't think I could walk either," said Anand looking back at the ugly woman. "You may want to bathe her." *In makeup*.

The two basketball players stayed with Nefertiti as Anand followed limping Tutankhaman. He realized he could out run the crippled kidnapper and escape in his rental car. "King Tut, you do know I could run to my car and leave you stranded."

"I know you won't."

"Why?"

"Because you're an archeologist that won't pass up one of the greatest historical events of the 21st century." Tutankhaman then stopped and turned around. "I know where your King Piankhi is buried."

"In Sudan, we call him King Piye and how did you know I was looking for him?"

"You are Nubian and the son of Timbuku. He was guided like many others by us to search for the *Gates of Shabaka.* We thought it was a tomb that held King Piankhi's treasures including the missing Ankhs. You were the only one to succeed in finding one." Anand didn't believe him. "During the time of King Piankhi when he invaded Egypt, he confiscated two of four Ankhs and deemed them gifts from the god Amun. He later had them plated in gold for his two favorite wives and as time passed the Ankhs disappeared."

"In many hieroglyphs," said Anand thinking of the pretty one. "Queen Nefertiti and other females are seen carrying the Ankh's."

"My mother used the Ankh to heal minor health problems in the sarcophagus and to communicate with our off-land safe-haven. (Atlantis) Each one has several functions and we only needed one to help us get home."

Chapter 10

Wooden Staffs

"How will you be getting home?" asked Anand. Tutankhaman didn't answer him.

"Stay and help us, and later you will be the most famous archeologist in the world."

"I don't want to be famous…I just want to find my King Piye and return him to Sudan."

"If I give you proof, will you help us?"

"Maybe."

"In your studies in the United States, did you learn about the lost tomb of Gilgamesh?"

"Yes, he was a king in Iraq…famous because of a book." Anand paused in thought. "He also ruled a city called Uruk."

"My dad said…because he was a good friend to our leader, we helped him build that city."

"Bull shit," coughed Anand.

"Before our *ship* left this planet, it destroyed the entire abandoned city of Uruk. The upper level was flattened, but deep under the city remains some of our labs and temporary living quarters."

"Why was the city destroyed?"

"To hide the advanced building techniques that would have change your history."

Mud brick buildings isn't high tech. Thought Anand. *I am visiting that city.*

"In 2005, I was notified that an Australian expedition team was on its way to Saqqara Egypt. I knew King Piankhi was buried there."

"Who removed him from his pyramid in El Kurru?" asked Anand.

"It was his son Taharqa. When the Assyrians were advancing south into Nubia and destroying everything, Taharqa had him moved to a secret location west of the El Kurru Pyramids. We found him after the Persians invaded and moved him to Saqqara. We knew your father's quest was to find King Pianki and his treasure…we hoped included the Ankhs."

"You *rhino humpers*…you just used my whole family only to find your precious key."

"We needed help in finding just one."

"I don't believe you have King Piye."

"When I heard the news of the expedition, I beat the Australians to the dig site. I removed King Piankhi's mummy and hid it under the flatten city of Uruk." Tutankhaman then opened his cell phone and displayed a picture of a mummy wearing a gold crown with two snakes in the front. "You do know what the two snakes represent?"

"Yes…the ruler of two lands."

"Your king is still in Iraq…and if you help us, I will tell you the coordinates of his exact location."

"I'll help, but that could be any mummy with a gold crown."

"The Sudanese Museum will prove it's him with x-rays and DNA comparison testing from other family members. Now…will you help us?"

"I will."

"Good, drive me to the three *Pyramids of the Queens*."

"Are they on the other side of the small pyramid Menkaure?"

"Yes."

Anand, as requested stopped 10 meters (33 Feet) from the second *Queens Pyramids* that very few tourists visited. The rental car caused a cloud of sand to rise and settle slowly as Tutankhaman opened the door and began limping toward the deteriorated middle pyramid. "Follow me," he shouted back at Anand. Tutankhaman climbed up three levels like a boy scout on cocaine being chased by his scoutmaster.

He better not be climbing to the top? Thought Anand as he struggled to get up on the first level. Tutankhaman reached into his pocket and pulled what looked like a square black crystal box.

He then placed it on the vertical flat surface of the limestone block. It began to recede and then open like the hood of BMW convertible. Tutankhaman walked into the opening as Anand reached the second level. "Grab these," echoed Tutankhaman as two long wooden staffs began to poke from the opening.

"I knew it," shouted Anand. "These poles are for picking up that heavy sarcophagus."

"Yes," said Tutankhaman as he held the other end.

We are going to need more men. Thought Anand as he began to slowly hop down the pyramid. *I'm not losing my nuts for that beautiful alien bitch with the 3000 year old pussy*. He then shoved the two long staffs into the open back window of the Land Cruiser.

"I need you to drive to the *Valley of the Kings*," ordered Tutankhaman.

"We may need some help," suggested Anand.

"My people are already there."

"Good."

Anand drove Tutankhaman above the speed limit down the Giza-Luxor Highway that eventually changed into the Cairo Road to Western Aswan. They reached the *Valley of the Kings* an hour before the sun set. As they drove toward the entrance gate, the guard nodded his head as he electrically opened a large fence. "Take me to KV-65."

"I am," said Anand. "I've been there and got a taste of your Viagra enhanced crowns." Tutankhaman smiled.

As they drove up to the guarded entrance of the unknown tomb, Anand's eyes opened wide in disbelief. The two tall men were standing next to the guard. "You had me drive for three hours while your basketball buddies probably flew here in a helicopter."

"They didn't fly," said Tutankhaman. "Maybe a little."

One of the seven foot giants grabbed the two wooden poles from the back of the Land Cruiser as Tutankhaman walked toward the entrance of the unknown tomb. The Egyptian guard opened the locked gate and then bowed on one knee with his head facing the sand. Anand followed and as he past the guard, he giggled before saying in English.

"Rise…my son." The guard stood up with an angry look on his face as he eyeballed Anand as if he was a white American. They walked to the chamber that tested the crowns and Tutankhaman picked up the red one first. "I wouldn't put that on your head if I was you," warned Anand. "You'll walk out of here with a raging boner."

"What's that?" asked Tutankhaman.

"Your willy," pointed Anand.

"I don't have one of those."

"Where you F.G.M.ed?"

"What?"

"Circumcised like a Muslim girl."

"Oh, you're talking about Female Genital Mutilation," said Tutankhaman. "That barbaric act of removing a female's clitoris so she won't have the urge to cheat is a custom we hate on this planet." (True)

"So…what happened to your love-stick?"

"I was born deformed and it was removed."

"I am so sorry."

"Why?"

"Because, you have to sit when you pee and can't fuck your sister."

Anand loved making funny comments about his new ancient friends. Tutankhaman began to sulk as he placed his black crystal on the inside seam of the crown. It began to smolder with smoke and Anand knew he was burning away the internal circuits.

After destroying all the crowns, both men entered the chamber that housed the sarcophagus as one of the giants layed the staffs next to each side of it. Tutankhaman pulled out the golden Ankh and placed it on the indentation of the sarcophagus. Only one eye began to glow.

"Just as I predicted, we have to get her to the surface," said Tutankhaman. "Into the sun."

"You big guys lift her up," ordered Anand. "And I'll make sure the chamber hall is clear." *Because I'm not losing my nuts like your boss.*

"We all have to lift a corner," said Tutankhaman. "For safety reasons."

Tutankhaman kneeled near the center of each staff and opened a concealed square section. Two buttons where exposed, one an intensity knob that he turned three times. The poles began to hum like a small jet turbine and then they all lifted. The magnetically attached staffs that connected through the entire sarcophagus caused it to only weigh 100 pounds (45 kilograms).

"I knew those pyramids weren't built with ropes and pulleys," said Anand.

"The stones *were* moved by black Hebrew slaves," said Tutankhaman. "We only helped them under the blind eye of night and in the day time, they lifted the limestone blocks by conventional means."

"And how did they do that?"

"Only with motivational ass whippings."

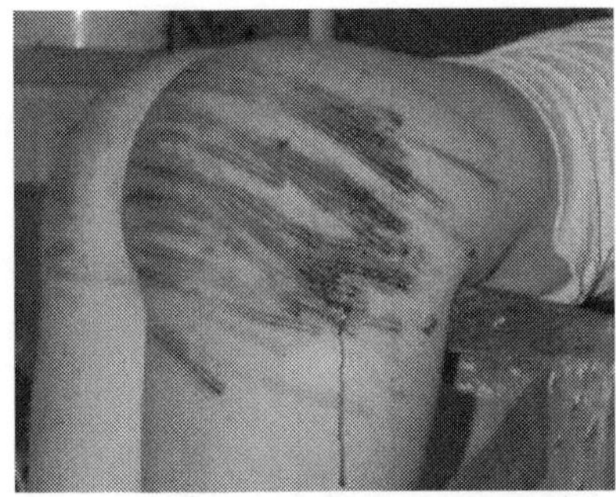

All four men carried the sarcophagus out of the tomb entrance as the guard held the door open. The sun was still shining as Anand turned to Tutankhaman.

"How long does it take for this thing to charge?" he asked. "I'm hungry, I stink, and I need a nap." Tutankhaman pulled out the black crystal and walked toward Anand.

"Just stand still, this won't hurt." The black crystal began to glow as he held it on the right side of Anand's head. "You are not hungry…you are not sleepy," recited Tutankhaman. "And you do not smell." Anand fell off balanced a little and then stood firmly.

"Wow…I feel as if I ate a whole Sudanese goat. And I'm not sleepy anymore." He then raised his armpit and took a deep breath. "I do smell like a Bangkok whore who just fucked ten men at one time."

"Do you smell sexy?" asked Tutankhaman.

"No, that's not what I meant. I smell like hippo sperm mixed with tuna fish."

"The *Gube* has strengthened your sense of smell."

"Please…take it away, that guard over there smells like my grandmother's hairy pussy…after she died." Tutankhaman then placed the *Gube* on the left side of Anand's skull while pressing a corner that caused it to glow and pulse yellow.

"How was that?"

"It worked and now I'm hungry for vagina scented Thai food served with cervical mucus dumplings smothered in a creamy *Vagisil* white sauce."

"I don't know what that means, but you can leave as soon as you drive me back to the Giza pyramids, to return the poles. Then I will tell you the exact location of your King Piankhi in Uruk. "

"You can tell me now."

"Later," said Tutankhaman feeling a little agitated. "The recharging of the sarcophagus only takes a couple of minutes and then we'll leave."

"Tell me how it works?"

"You won't understand."

"Is it how you traveled to Earth?"

"My parents did. I was born here." Anand tried to catch him in a lie.

"If I sat in that thing, will I live forever?"

"You won't, your Einstein was 28 years old when he died of old age."

"Damn."

"It did increase his intelligence."

"I'd rather be young with a hard dick than smart."

The sun was dim from setting below the desert horizon when Tutankhaman walked and kneeled next to the sarcophagus. He placed the golden Ankh on the indented spot again and both eyes began to glow.

"It is ready," said Tutankhaman. The seams of the limestone lid appeared again and then it opened slowly. The naked body of the beautiful Queen Kiya began to move as she took a deep breath.

She is making me horny. Thought Anand as he only stared at her hairy vagina. She then sat up as the setting sun radiated her brown skin like a newborn child. One of the giants placed a blanket over her shoulders that looked like a so-called Negroe Hebrew slave (*From the Lost Tribe of Judah*) knitted three thousand years ago. The other grabbed the anti-gravity poles and threw them into the back of the rental car.

"She can ride with us," suggested Anand, only to ask her questions.

"She is riding in another vehicle."

"Is it a space ship?"

"No, it's a modified cruiser that rides above the sand and uses the surface heat to hide from satellites."

"I knew you had something that hid from the government."

"We needed you to drive because the power in the poles interferes with the cruiser's cloaking field."

"Can you take me to Iraq?" asked Anand only wanting to ride in the cruiser. "To bring back my king."

"I will take you."

Four hours later, they arrived at the *Giza Pyramids* and Anand looked confused as he got out of the car.

"So you're saying during World War II, you stopped Hitler from making his own Atomic bomb, implanted in Nikola Tesla's mind the idea to invent alternating current, and used a long range gravity beam to reversed course the Russian ships in 1962 that carried nuclear weapons to Cuba?"

"Yes, we prevented your world from being destroyed numerous times."

"If you can do that," asked Anand. "Then why didn't you stop the meteor that caused the *Medieval Ice Age* in the 1700's? It changed the climate all over the world."

"How did you know it was a meteor?" asked Tutankhaman stopping in his steps. "In your history volcanoes and changing ocean currents were the cause."

"In college, I learned that archaeological expeditions in France close to the English Channel revealed a number of people during that time period died from bone marrow radiation."

Tutankhaman smirked and hesitated to speak. "England and France's coastlines were joined together before the meteor hit in the Atlantic Ocean. We were unable to stop it because of the Ottoman Wars. The battles were too large for us to fight and eventually the Ottoman Empire ruled over Egypt and Syria." Tutankhaman began to stutter. "We…I mean my people had to evacuate our underground complex below Uruk that housed the *Repulsor*."

"You're lying," shouted Anand as he tapped on his cell phone and accessed the internet. "You wanted the population decreased. It says here that the Great Northern War of numerous European countries was fought during most of the 1700's and…and the bubonic plague mysteriously had another outbreak shortly thereafter."

“We had to find a way of stopping the violence without being seen.”

“So you let the meteor hit and placed infected rats onboard trading ships heading back to Europe.” Anand paused in thought. “Answer this last question?” he asked while carrying the two anti-gravity poles. “Do you aliens…only hate white people, like African Americans?”

“The frequency of violence is continuous amongst the causation race of Europe compared to other counties.” Tutankhaman then stepped on the first level of limestone on the *Queens Pyramid* and turned toward Anand. “They seem to advance quickly in making tools that kill. And we knew that would be a threat as the centuries passed.”

“That is no lie,” said Anand while passing up both poles. “Those sheep-fuckers are good at killing.”

“What’s a sheep-fucker?”

“People…mostly Arabs who have sex with farm animals, preferably goats.”

“My men say female chimpanzees are quite pleasurable,” responded Tutankhaman.

They probably started the Aids epidemic,” thought Anand. *I’m calling P.E.T.A*, *when I get back to Sudan. After hearing this shit, Michael Jackson must be turning over in his grave. Fucking monkey molesters.*

Chapter 11

The APC

Tutankhaman jumped from the pyramid as Anand turned toward the sound of a jet engine getting closer. “Our ride has arrived,” said Tutankhaman. A desert beige ***Armored Personnel Carrier*** turned the corner of the pyramid and stopped in front of the men.

“The Egyptian Army is giving us a ride into Iraq?” asked Anand. “I’ll pass on that suicidal trip.”

“The shell of that truck was taken only to not draw attention.”

“What was it before?” asked Anand, while thinking about Tutankhaman’s past. “A two wheeled flying chariot.”

“It’ll only take twenty minutes to get to Uruk.”

"Didn't you say it was in Iraq?" asked Anand. "Which is about two thousand kilometers (1300 miles) away?"

"Yes."

Anand grabbed his backpack, stepped onto the vehicle, and then his mouth dropped open again. The interior was that of a future airliner and the driver's console looked like something out of Star Wars.

One of the giants sat on the right to drive as Tutankhaman sat on the left. "This is amazing," said Anand.

"You may want to buckle up." The vehicle then hummed and moved forward as it drove onto the rough bumpy desert.

"Your advanced truck rides as smooth as my rental on the streets of Cairo," Anand said sarcastically. "My already hand raped asshole doesn't need to be juggled around unless you have a pillow I could sit on."

Five minutes later, as they were far enough from the Egyptian pyramids, the engine began to sound like an airliner just about to takeoff. The carrier rose ten feet (three meters) off the sand surface and then the wheels retracted. "Did you steal the technical plans from Lockheed?"

"What plans?" asked Tutankhaman.

"I feel as if I flew on this plane on the way to Berlin." The vehicle then accelerated up to ***Mark Ten*** in two minutes (Ten times the speed of sound). The desert was flashing by the small windows as Anand was amazed. "My father would have loved a ride in this."

"Timbuku did," said Tutankhaman. "When he was a boy riding a camel, we followed him taking a wrong turn into open desert. We had to drug…him and his friend then transport them close to Al Dabbah."

"Where did you put the camel?" asked Anand. "On the roof."

"We ate him and purchased another one from the city," said Tutankhaman. "Our people love camel grogs smothered in onions."

I hope he's not talking about the camel's nuts. Thought Anand. "I've read that most pharaohs of early Egypt had bad teeth. They chewed bread with sand mixed in with the grain and ate dates that had hard seeds."

"I miss the Semolina sweet cakes of that time period," reminisced Tutankhaman.

"I miss that old woman," smiled Anand. "And the softness of her flat titties."

Tutankhaman quickly looked back. "Did you put the T.T.C. (Thought Transference Crown) on again before I disabled it?"

"No," said Anand.

"Then…why do you have a ferret in your pants trying to escape." Anand looked down and he had another boner.

"Can you use that crystal again?" asked Anand as the giant smiled. "It is causing me to have uncontrollable thoughts and feelings?" Tutankhaman unsnapped his seatbelt and sat next to Anand.

"The side effect you are experiencing now is what the Americans call...blue balls."

"My nuts are fucking green and I'm only horny for Nefertiti," said Anand. "The ugly one." Tutankhaman frowned.

"The crown you put on was my father's…Akhenaten. It has somehow residually transferred his L.M.E (Libido Mind Enhancement) patterns to you," said Tutankhaman. "It was the only way for him to make love to my mother."

"Don't forget…she's your aunt too."

"Close your eyes." Anand hesitated while rubbing his nuts.

"What is that black box going to do to me this time?" he asked.

"It will put you to sleep momentarily and when you awake, you should be back to normal."

Anand rested his head back and Tutankhaman placed a different object on his head. Anand fell into a deep sleep and began snoring. He believed fifteen minutes had past when he awakened with a long drool spot down his shirt. He looked up as the carrier began to slow down in speed.

"Are we in Iraq?" Anand asked with a smile.

"No, we are in Sudan."

"Sudan," Anand said surprisingly. "How long was I asleep?"

"One hour and thirty five minutes." Anand looked to the back of the truck and King Piankhi's mummy was on a stretcher wrapped in a special clear plastic.

"Thank you so much," Anand said gratefully. "Our king can truly rest in peace in his homeland of Nubia."

"Do you wish to join us as we power up the Khufu (Giza) Pyramid?" asked Tutankhaman as the truck wheels began to lower.

"I have to get King Piye to a safe place."

"My loyal friend in Khartoum will deliver the mummy," said Tutankhaman. "To the National Museum of Sudan."

"I don't trust anybody when it comes to this priceless treasure." The truck then rolled off the sand and onto a paved road.

"I already called my friend and I would trust him with my life," said Tutankhaman.

"What life," stated Anand in a high tone. "You will never die." Tutankhaman dialed his cell phone as the truck sped down a long highway road and then stopped.

"We're here," said Tutankhaman then pausing before ending the call. "Canuk open the door," he ordered. All three men got out as a distant car was approaching from a different direction.

"My friend is here." The brown Ford Explorer finally stopped and Anand's brother exited the driver's seat.

"Kintu!" yelled Anand as he began to quickly walk toward him. He excitingly held up his arms when he saw Nafy exit from the back passenger door. Anand began to cry and quickly ran past his brother to his fiancée. He picked her up by the butt cheeks and kissed her passionately.

"I missed you too little brother," sarcastically said Kintu as he shook Tutankhaman's soft hand. Anand walked back toward the cruiser while hugging Nafy.

"Kintu, how long have you known Tutankhaman?"

"It was when Dad became rich. Tutankhaman told me to keep it a secret until you found King Piye."

"Did Tut also help you find Dad's friend Suni?"

"Yes, they followed him and Dad most of their lives including Grandpa Zula. I knew you were with them so I brought Nafy."

"Thank you," said Anand. "Do you know they just used our whole family? They only wanted the golden Ankh to release Nefertiti from a deep sleep and to send a signal into space."

"I didn't know they were looking for the Ankh," said Kintu. "And please tell me she is beautiful as her pictures?"

"Hell…no," said Anand while shrugging. "She is bat shit ugly."

"Dad told us the Atlantians contacted him when he sold the gold plate to the Germans. They told us Shabaka's treasure would lead to King Piye being returned to Sudan."

"These people are from Atlantis?" asked Anand.

"My mother built the city you humans call Atlantis," stated Tutankhaman. "Until we sunk and hid it under the ocean." An alarm sounded on the ***AP*** carrier as the giant walked quickly and removed the mummy of King Piankhi.

"We have to go," shouted Tutankhaman.

"Place the king in the back of the Explorer," said Kintu.

"Come with us Nafy," asked Anand.

"Where?"

"To Egypt, they're going to power up the Giza Pyramid."

"Okay."

"Big brother, take care of our king," shouted Anand, before getting back into the loud starting carrier.

"I will."

Four miles out, an American armed drone was heading in their direction. U.S satellites had picked up the fast moving sand contrails but not the transport vehicle itself. The drone was sent to investigate the last known position.

"We have to find shelter to hide or speed to a military base," said Tutankhaman. "This will alert them that a new high speed military vehicle is being tested in this country."

"I don't want the United States in my country and then later setting up a network of undercover spies."

"We can return to Egypt," said Tutankhaman.

"Let's go to Iran," suggested Anand. "They are already put on a high surveillance level."

"We'll stop there and then under the cover of night slowly return to Giza."

"Will they be serving dinner and a movie on this flight?" asked Nafy.

"Yes," said Tutankhaman who became hungry. "We are having fried camel *Grogs* smothered in a spicy onion gravy over Koshari (A mixture of rice, lentil, and macaroni noodles.).

"I'm not hungry anymore," said Anand knowing *Grogs* was testicles. The sound of a missile was suddenly heard before it exploded near the rear of the carrier. Nafy became scared as the hi-tech truck shook from the shockwave. Then it floated and retracted its wheels. "It's two American F-22's," shouted Anand as he spotted them from the front window.

"They only wanted to slow us down," said Tutankhaman. "To capture this vehicle." The truck began to speed up as the F-22's followed. Then the truck reached ***Mach-Five*** and both jets were matching their speed.

"I knew the F-22 was fast, but not that fast," said Anand. Then the truck began to lose the jets, reaching ***Mach-Nine*** thirty seconds later.

"We are on our way to Dezful Airbase in Iran," said the giant.

"So they *can* talk," stated Anand. "What's his real name?"

"Zaqelizeta," said Tutankhaman. "His Earthly name is Canuk."

"Hey Canuk…can you ball?"

"I can't mate with humans."

"I'm talking about playing basketball not humping monkeys?"

"No, running is forbidden."

"Why are you forbidden to run?" asked Nafy.

"It's our bones," said Canuk.

"Tutankhaman is that why you are limping?" asked Anand.

"Yes and no."

"What happened?" asked Nafy.

"He's a talker," said Anand. "Sit back because this is going to be a long story."

Chapter 12

The Signal

"After World War II ended," said Tutankhaman while sitting next to Nafy. "Egypt became another Argentina and allowed escaping Nazis to enter the country. King Farouk at the time hired them as military, financial, and technical advisors. (True)

One Nazi, a Dr. Aribert Heim believed a rumor about my people and was obsessed with capturing me only. One year in Cairo, I was followed to a metal fabrication shop. I think it was October of 1952 and three well-fit white men followed me as I entered. I continued walking and left out the back of the building. I turned to my right and another white man had just turned into the ally. He yelled a few words I didn't understand and I started running. My legs held up strong until I crossed the busy street. Then my ankle shattered like glass when I tripped and hit the edge of the sidewalk. I fell in pain and looked up. It was Dr. Aribert Heim standing over me and he said one word, 'Tutankhaman'. Then suddenly the other three men exited the shop and Dr. Heim ran with fear in his eyes. Those three men were from Israeli Intelligence and wanted to capture Dr. Heim, to have him stand trial for crimes against humanity. They took me to their safe-house and bandage my ankle until my people came and transported me home."

"With all of your high tech gadgets," said Nafy. "Why can't you fix your bones?"

"Remember, my mother and father were stranded here," stated Tutankhaman. "They had limited equipment to repair fractures."

"She didn't know that," said Anand.

"My father's legs were genetically recycled seven times in the ship's infirmary before it left this planet. Our bones seem to deteriorate because of this planets sun."

"It says here," said Anand while looking down at his cell phone. "Dr. Aribert Heim who was called Doctor Death, tortured Romani women in Mauthausen Austria and was never caught for his crimes." (True)

"We caught him," said Tutankhaman. "I have this second limp because of him and he had to pay."

"And he tasted delicious," said Canuk while looking back toward them.

I knew these alien motherfuckers ate people. Thought Anand, sounding like his black American college room-mate. "Just remember…Sudanese people *don't* taste like chicken."

"We only eat our enemies that do us harm."

So that's why they wrapped people into mummies like spiders. Thought Anand. *To eat them later.*

"I will be your friend for a long time," said Nafy, not wanting to be eaten.

"Yeah, eat me when I'm ninety six years old," said Anand while smiling. *When my dick stops working.*

The truck slowed down near Dezful Airbase in Iran and then headed in the direction of Egypt. "We have to slow our speed to conceal our heat signature and contrail from orbiting satellites," said Tutankhaman. "I'm sorry, but we have to turn up the coolers." He then opened a ceiling cabinet and gave Anand and Nafy each a 2000 year old Hebrew knitted blanket.

"Did this belong to Moses?" asked Anand as Nafy smiled.

"No," said Tutankhaman. "Canuk knitted them."

I knew that tall freak was gay. Thought Anand. *He smiled with envy when my dick was hard.*

The temperature dropped to forty three degrees Fahrenheit (six degrees Celsius) quickly. "Our bodies were designed to adjust to all temperatures within a certain limit," said Tutankhaman.

"Our dark skin protects us from the hot sun," said Anand. "And white people can withstand extreme cold temperatures, but sit in the hot sun and try to get black."

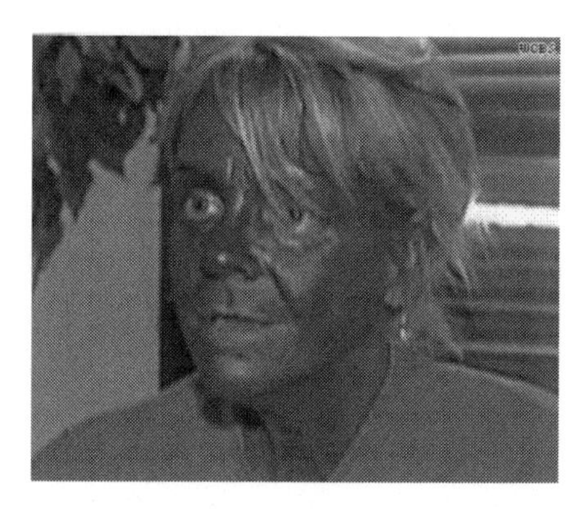

"It won't be long," said Tutankhaman. Nafy's teeth began to chatter from the cold as Canuk listened with amazement.

Ten minutes later, the truck slowed as it neared the Suez Canal. "Are we in Egypt?" ask Nafy.

"No, since we slowed our speed, we can't fly over water without being detected," said Tutankhaman. "The good news is…we are turning off the coolers."

"Listen!" yelled Canuk as he stopped the truck.

"I don't hear anything," said Nafy.

"Me nether," said Anand, only hearing humming from the carrier engine.

"It's a helicopter," said Tutankhaman. "An Israeli Apache eight kilometers out (five miles)."

“It is fully armed,” said Canuk.

“Go full speed to Khufu (Giza Pyramids),” ordered Tutankhaman.

They reached the middle of Egypt in record time as an arrival alarm beeped twice. The truck drove onto the main road that led toward the Giza Pyramids as the sun was setting. “We have to hurry,” said Tutankhaman. “I believe the Americans are tracking us.”

“They can’t send their military to an historic Egyptian site,” said Anand.

“The Americans have a secret base in the Egyptian desert and have been trying to capture us since we crashed a research test ship in Roswell. Our bio-constructed humanoids were going to the moon to set up an ocean mapping transponder.”

“Then speed this thing up,” said Nafy.

The truck drove quickly on the road as leaving tour buses passed them. Seven minutes later they drove up to the Khufu (Giza) Pyramid and all got out.

“Anand, pass me the triangle amulet from around your neck.”

"How did you know I had it?" asked Anand as he reached under his shirt collar.

"The *blue-balls* you experienced earlier was caused by the amulets power. We knew Kiya had it around her neck and when I scanned your body in the cruiser, I knew why you were rubbing your testicles. I didn't want you to remove it until we returned," said Tutankhaman while holding his hand out that had no finger print lines. "The electrical impulses of your body's synaptic nervous system maintained its energy level."

"You used me again," angrily said Anand. "Are we Earthlings just prostitutes for your sick space pimping way of doing things?"

"Many years ago, I would've had the flesh removed from your live body for talking to me that way."

"If I had bigger muscles and you weren't a cannibal…I'd kick your ass."

"We knew when you left for college in America, its violent culture would significantly influence your behavior."

"No, your arrogance is making me violent."

"Anand let it go," said Nafy. "His people have been stranded here for a long time."

"Me too…I hate fucking Egypt."

"Stay here with Canuk," ordered Tutankhaman. "If the military is a threat, he will take you to Atlantis."

"Where's is it?" asked Anand.

"It's hidden in the ocean, safe from you humans and your satellites."

"If it's at the North or South pole you can leave me and Nafy here," said Anand. "I'm not freezing my ass off anymore."

"Please take us to Sudan?" asked Nafy. "We will be safe in our own country."

"Maybe," said Tutankhaman. "Be patient."

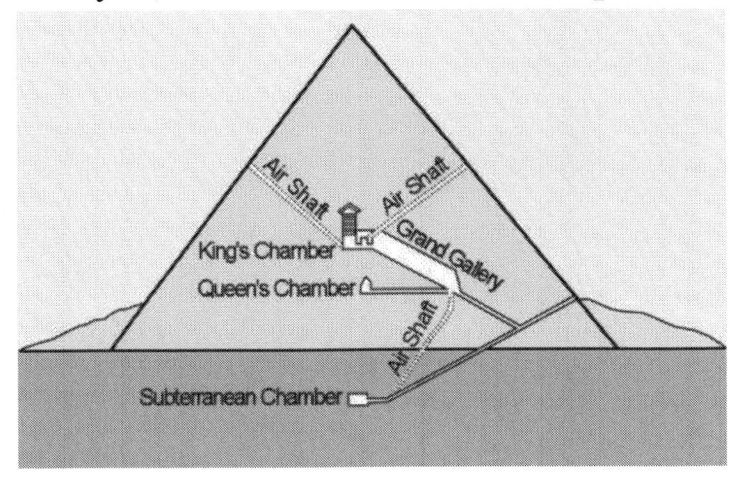

"How are you going to power up the pyramid?" asked Nafy.

"I have to reach the kings chamber in the center of the pyramid," said Tutankhaman. "Then place the T.A.R. (Trilateral Amulet of Ra.) ignition enabler on the tomb wall just above the sarcophagus. Once I reach the bottomless pit, I will light the fuse."

King's Chamber

"With fire?" asked Nafy.

"No, actually I will be opening a panel and starting the fusion amplifiers in the two smaller pyramids. They are connected to the subterranean chamber at the bottom of the Giza Pyramid and will shoot a focused beam of induced quasi and electrical plasma upward in the direction of our home world." Nafy looked confused as Anand looked up at the top of the pyramid. "In that focused beam will be a message in its stream informing my people that the technology on this planet has advanced enough for us to live comfortably after we take full control of it."

"You said your ship left the planet to answer an emergency signal from the *Pinir* midway station," stated Anand.

"Didn't I tell you…I was a habitual liar?" stated Tutankhaman. "There is no midway station. I learned to lie from a Greek philosopher named Plato. His writings were filled with untrue facts and myths like that crazy fuck Nostradamus. He also lied insisting Athen's wooden ships destroyed Atlantis and sunk her. Actually we submerged it into the ocean and move it after a volcano called Thera was falsely predicted to erupt.

"I knew you fuckers were evil," said Anand. "I could feel it in my bones."

"I have placed myself in charge and will rule this planet like my parents," said Tutankhaman. Canuk then grabbed Anand by the shoulders, not allowing him to move.

"Nafy, you are free to leave in Anand's truck. He will be released after the signal has been sent."

"I want to stay with him."

"Go Nafy," shouted Anand. "I'll be alright." *I knew I should've sold that Ankh.* He thought. "History warned me about you fucked up ancient Egyptians and I didn't listen."

"We ruled with fear and loved it," Tutankhaman said confidently. "And I want that feeling on a global scale."

"Even if you're king of this planet, you still can't fuck." Nafy smiled. "I know if I lost my dick…I would off myself with a gun. It's not too late."

"I'm gay," angrily said Tutankhaman.

"Oh my god, you're a catcher," said Anand.

"I hate American baseball."

"No…you like it up the ass."

"Lock him in the cruiser," angrily ordered Tutankhaman. Anand was being pulled as Nafy stood next to Tutankhaman.

Akhenaten

"I know what happened to your transgender dress wearing father Akhenaten," shouted Anand. "You wanted to be king so badly you killed him after entombing your ugly mother and his other wives in those sarcophagus's." Tutankhaman stopped and became extremely angry knowing he was telling the truth. "Then what you didn't expect was…losing the only two Ankh keys you had to the invading Persians and needing the others my King Piye took in the 25th dynasty."

Nafy then grabbed the T.A.R. triangle necklace from Tutankhaman's hand and ran.

"Get her!" he yelled as Canuk began to chase. Anand ran to the carrier, grabbed his cell phone, and dialed while picking up his backpack. Then he ran to his rented Toyota and drove with a purpose.

Canuk had captured Nafy, but he was limping back to the pyramid. He gave Tutankhaman the (Triangle Amulet of Ra) necklace and he began climbing the pyramid to reach the entrance.

Anand had driven around the entire pyramid with no headlights and suddenly beeped the horn frantically. Canuk turned around not realizing he released Nafy. She ran away from him as the Land Cruiser crashed into Canuk. It caused his already cracked legs to shatter and detach at the knees when he flew into the air. Tutankhaman entered the pyramid as one Egyptian guard's headlights were seen driving toward them in the dark distance. Anand picked up Nafy and drove slowly to the exit road. "I thought your scared punk ass left me," said Nafy in Arabic.

"I would never leave you with those nut eating aliens that consume camels and humans for breakfast."

The security guard's truck stopped in front of the Toyota as its high beams flashed. The same guard that let him in the gate exited from his passenger side. He walked up to Anand's window with a flashlight.

"We were coming to get you," said Anand. "Master Tut needs to get in KV-65. The gate is locked."

"You have to leave now," said the guard in Arabic. "A sand storm is coming."

"Oh…it sure is." Anand drove at a steady speed and when they exited the main gate the ground began to shake. He stopped the Land Cruiser and they both got out.

"Look at the pyramid," said Nafy in amazement. "It's glowing yellow."

"It won't be for long," said Anand. "I called my black American college roommate who works at the U.S. Pentagon."

"What is he going to do?" asked Nafy.

"I don't know. But I told him in five minutes, that if they didn't blow up the pyramid and the truck they've been tracking, we will be invaded and enslaved by advanced white people from another planet."

Then the pyramid began to glow bright red. The ground shook harder and then a sparkle of light as bright as the sun shot into the air and floated.

The entire area lit up in daylight. Then the sparkle exploded in a rainbow of colors as a blue and white steady pulsating beam shot from the pyramid top and into space. At that very moment Nafy pointed upward.

"Look Anand!"

Two American F-15 fighters were in full afterburner heading toward the pyramid. One released a *Bunker Buster* guided bomb as the other fired a *Sidewinder* missile.

The bomb crashed into the pyramid without making a sound. Then the *Sidewinder* blew up the high tech armored personnel carrier as the guards were picking up Canuk's legs. The beam stopped pulsating as smoke began to rise from the entrance and vent holes of the pyramid.

"Let's get out of here," frantically said Nafy. "You hit Canuk with the car and they're going to eat you."

Anand drove southbound all night towards Sudan. He used illegal smuggling roads knowing Tutankhaman and his loyal Egyptian officials would be looking for them at the border.

The next day, they were national heroes in Sudan and the word spread. The people of his home country including some Egyptians offered them gas, food, and sometimes a place to rest as they journeyed home back to Khartoum.

Two days later, Anand finally stopped the Toyota Land Cruiser in front of Nafy's house.

"So what you're saying is," stated Nafy. "Tutankhaman gave out a bunch of wooden boxes full of priceless artifacts including the one to your grandfather...only to get Timbuku interested in archaeology."

"Yes, except the small replica of Shabaka's Stone was a fake."

"Then Tut had you followed after Timbuku gave you all his research papers, hoping you would find clues to the whereabouts of the four missing Ankhs."

"This mess all started with the German tour guide," said Anand then lying. "He informed the Egyptian mob that I found and stole the golden Ankh from the museum."

"Tutankhaman then persuaded you to help him by giving you King Piyes mummy."

"I think he liked and respected the Nubians 3000 years ago for not killing his father and ugly mother Nefertiti." Anand then frowned while remembering her face. "He also knew how important it was for the Sudanese people to have their king returned."

"Do you think Tutankhaman is dead?" she asked.

"No, I believe he escaped from the pyramid," said Anand who was tired.

"At least his signal wasn't sent."

"I don't think it matters," said Anand. "He lied so much I don't believe anything he told us." He then paused for a second. "And why would he send a signal to his home-world?"

"Maybe he was telling the truth and sent an invasion invitation," said Nafy. Anand almost agreed.

"We don't know what or where that message was being sent. Let's just hope the Americans stopped it in time."

"I hope so," said Nafy. "I don't like cannibals…except you."

"We'll find out in twenty years."

"What?" asked Nafy.

"He said it would take their ship twenty years to get here."

"We are going to be prepared if that happens."

"I think I know why their ship hasn't returned," said Anand. "Tutankhaman's people are us…from the future. I figured they may have entered a black hole and slipped into our past."

"Did you bump your head?"

"How come they are human?" asked Anand.

"I don't know and don't care," said Nafy a little worried. "That little cripple tried to send a message to someone and in twenty years, we better be ready for anything."

"If my black hole theory is correct, nothing will happen," said Anand. "Then he'll probably try a different plan to conquer the world."

"He won't have a big enough army by then," said Nafy.

"What he does have is immortality," said Anand. "And all the time in the world to recruit."

The End.

Page 43

In 1350 BC, Akhenaten had the reacquired golden Ankh incased in between the Home Altar tablet. It was a spare master key hidden only to be broken open in case of an emergency.

(Not True)

To the Readcr

I never knew there was a black pharaoh who ruled Egypt until 2008. I've read about Egyptian pyramids in public school, but was never told about the Kush people in Nubia (Sudan) that also built pyramids. There is a lot of black history out there intentionally being withheld especially from the Israelite African Americans. (Read my book TIM, The Lost Slaves)

Uncensored title is singular, *The Lost Slave*.

During and before the *Civil Rights Movement* many African American's were not acknowledged for their contributions in the development of the country. I've mentioned a few "tokens" that made it into American school books; Crispus Attucks, Benjamin Banneker, Frederick Douglas, and Mathew Henson.

Crispus Attucks (1723-1770) was at the wrong place…at the wrong time. He was considered the first and only black man (Taught in schools.) to die for the American Revolution. (100,000 blacks actually died)

Eight British soldiers fired their muskets into a crowd and were later acquitted for murder because of their lawyer pleading self defense. That lawyer was John Adams who later became the second President of the United States.

Benjamin Banneker (1731-1806) was a self taught scientist that used his memory from the charts of a disgruntled French architect and designed the capital of Washington D.C. His white grandmother immigrated to America with two of her slaves and secretly married one of them. Her daughter was Benjamin's mother.

Frederick Douglas (1818-1895) was an abolitionist against slavery whose father was white. This made northerners sympathetic and allowed him to write and give speeches on inequality. In 1845, he wrote his autobiography because people mostly white didn't believe he was a former slave. He later became famous for his writings that endangered his freedom. Being half white, he fled to Liverpool England for two years.

Mathew Henson (1866-1955) was the first African America to reach the North Pole in 1909. He assisted Robert Peary on the expedition and learned to speak the language of the *Inuit* people (Eskimos). It is disputed, (Only because a black man was on the expedition.) that a Dr. Frederick Cook and his team reached the North Pole first a year earlier.

Many Blacks have contributed over the years in American society and have not been mentioned throughout its history. Here are a few I've honorably mentioned below.

Frederick Jones Inventor of the air conditioner
Sarah Boone: Invented the ironing board.
Henry Blair: Invented a better spark plug.
Oscar brown: Improved the horse shoe.
David Crosthwait: Invented a shoe assembly machine.
Garett Morgan: Invented the first traffic signal.

Lloyd Quarterman*:* Worked on the Manhattan Project. (Development of the *Little Boy* Atomic Bomb)
Ernest Wilkins*:* Also worked on the Manhattan Project.
Granville Woods*:* Invented the synchronous Multiplex Railway telegraph.
Alice Ball: Chemist that invented an injectable oil of Chaulmoogra for the treatment of Leprosy.
Charles Chappelle*:* Designed an airplane for long distance flight.
George Washington Carver *invented peanut butter.*

"Time is the enemy in obtaining all truths."

Michael K. Jones

Michael's other Books

Read my other 10 novels that are funny.

Tim was written only for so-called African Americans.

kylesarmy@gmail.com

Page 27-28

The Rockefeller Dime Toss

Rockefeller reference of true event.

Documentary

Rise from the Rail:

The story of the Pullman Porter. (2006)
Based on the bestselling book by Larry Tye.

Become an Author and Screenwriter

Learn to write and sell your own novel and screenplay.

This instruction manual has step by step instructions with sample pages to help you from beginning-to-end on how to complete your first novel.

It is also filled with information on how to write a screenplay. I've added website links that will help you find a literary agent including how to self-publish your book almost for free. Check out the sample pages of all my books on Amazon especially *Profiling or Prejudice*.

Made in the USA
Monee, IL
31 May 2020

32259055R00104